MW01125894

Gabriel's Promise
By Jordan Silver

Copyright © 2013 Alison Jordan

All Rights Reserved

Table of Contents

Chapter 1

Samantha Holder is a handful. Anyone who knows her knows the hellcat would as soon spit in your eye as shake your hand. She had the gumption of ten men and a mean streak a mile wide. That was of course if you were stupid enough to get on her bad side and pretty much everyone was the enemy except Charlie Holder. Chief Holder tried to do his best by his only surviving child after losing his son Phillip in the war when Sam as she preferred to be called was just twelve.

Now Phillip was the only one who could curtail little Miss. Spitfire. According to the doting big brother she just needed a guiding hand. What she needed was a swift kick to the backside and that's that. No one had been able to control her since her brother's demise. Who am I you ask, oh nobody really, just Delilah Spelman, town librarian and unofficial historian. I was born and raised in these parts and I know the comings and goings of pretty much everyone around here. That's how I knew trouble was brewing when I saw the fancy Hollywood type in his fancy sports car pull up outside the Holder residence. I hope to God he wasn't a salesman or something. The last one of them Samantha had sent packing with Charlie's old shotgun.

That must've been a good three months ago and we hadn't had any shenanigans since then so I guess we were due. I headed out to my porch with my afternoon libation to watch the fireworks.

SAM

I saw the fancy man in his fancy car when he pulled up outside, I was watching from my upstairs bedroom window. He looked vaguely familiar but I couldn't quite place him. Probably seen him on the TV though what a highfalutin television star would be doing in Lexington New

York was beyond me. No one came to Lexington unless they were lost.

Well anyway like I said, he looked vaguely familiar. I hope he wasn't selling anything cause there wasn't anything I hated more than a snake oil salesman, pretty or not if I didn't like what he had to say I would just run him off with my dad's trustee shotgun. That always did the trick.

GABE

This trip was long overdue and I felt the familiar pang of sorrow at the loss of my old friend once more when I took my first look at his childhood home. The place could do with some repairs maybe I'd look into that first, a little paint and maybe some new shutters. Looking around it wasn't in much different shape to its neighbors but still it's something my old buddy would've wanted. From what I could remember Phil's dad had been the chief of police here in Lexington, population eight hundred, until a freak accident had left him in a wheelchair when Phil was seventeen and his sister Samantha eight.

Phil had already enlisted and couldn't get out of it for some obscure reason or other, so when he had been called up four years later he had left his then twelve- year old sister at home with their dad. If I remembered the stories Phil had liked to regale me with about his precocious little sister, she had opted for homeschooling so she could be home to help out with their dad, since their mother had died giving birth to her.

I could still envision the toothy little urchin in pigtails. Phil had carried that picture with him everywhere. I'd been unable to attend his funeral seeing as how I was in a coma at the time. When I was finally released some three months later after extensive therapy that had helped to get me back in tip-top shape after a bullet had shattered my femur he was long in the ground. I'd had other wounds from the shrapnel that pierced my body, but that had been the worst. The docs didn't hold out much hope of me walking again, but they didn't know my will. The Sweeney strength of will was legendary.

Within six months not only was I walking, but in another three the limp was gone. After I made a full recovery I was officially discharged from the army at the ripe old age of twenty-two. That's when my grandpa had his near fatal heart attack and it was left to me to take over the reigns. Dad had no head for business so it skipped a generation and fell to me. My older brother by two years Jonathan also had no interest in the business arena, preferring to be a professional football player instead.

I put on my ray bans as I exited the car, hoping it wasn't too late to keep my promise, late in coming as I was.

Chief

I sure hope this fool wasn't here to sell anything; I was in no mood to save another backside from my infuriating daughter's buckshot.

I should just put up a sign, 'Strangers beware of rabid teenager', that would sure save me a lot of aggravation. As the young man drew closer to the front where I was hiding out behind the window I got a good look at his face. Well now what have we here? It was about damn time, I was getting tired of keeping my little hellion in line, looked like the Calvary had finally arrived. It had only taken him six years but better later than never is what I say.

Chapter 2

GABE

It was pretty quiet for the middle of the day, and I wondered as I walked up to the door if maybe I should've called before I came. Well, it was too late for second guessing myself now, besides the door opened as I reached the top step. " Hello Gabriel."

"Sir?" I was sure because of the wheelchair that this had to be Charlie Holder, but how the hell did he know who I was?
"I recognize you boy, from the pictures my son used to send home." He had a wistful look for just a moment at the mention of Phillip.
Of course, how could I forget, Phil and his damn snapshots, he had been determined to make a scrapbook for his little Sammy. I'd completely forgotten all about that.

Reaching out my hand I came back to the present. "It's a pleasure to finally meet you sir."

We shook hands and I could've sworn he grumbled something like "It's about damn time." "Sorry?"

"Nothing son just clearing my throat." He made the universal sound of throat clearing. "Come on in son." He wheeled around and led me deeper into the living room. The place was neat but threadbare and I felt a pang of guilt, how could I have gone six years without keeping my promise? The least I could've done in all that time was make a phone call, but I'd been so busy with my life I'd let down a friend, I'd broken my word. Charlie wheeled himself to the bottom of the stairs.

"Sam honey we have company." Did he just roll his eyes, looked like chief Holder was a bit eccentric.
"Samantha Eliza Holder get down these stairs." He didn't quite yell but it was close, I was about to tell him it was okay, I could wait but then she answered.
"I'm coming pop, keep your shirt on." There was some stomping around and grumbling coming from above and I didn't know whether to laugh or frown when Charlie started grumbling again.

"And he better not be another one of those salesmen we don't need no vacuum cleaners, we have no use for high speed Internet and let me see, what else are they selling these days? Whatever, whatever it is we don't need it, so if he's here for that you better get rid of him before I get down there, that's all I'm saying."

"Sam..." now he was shouting.
"I'm sorry about that son, I raised her better than that she's just having an off day; I'm sure my son told you all about little Sam, she didn't have a mom poor little thing, so it was just me and her brother and I'm afraid she's kind of rougher around the edges than most girls."
"Pop I can hear you and why the blazes are you discussing me with a complete and total stranger anyway?"
Wow, she sounded like a real shrew, I hope I was going to be able to fulfill my promise, but I had no tolerance for shrewish behavior. The stomping finally reached the head of the stairs before it sounded like a stampede was descending.
This little ball of fire flew down the stairs, long legs, hair in a wild abundance of curls down to her ass and what an ass it was.
"I'm here now what?" She turned to me.

Oh my fucking word, I think my dick just took a bow. She was fucking magnificent.

Chapter 3

GABE

Have mercy, this couldn't be her could it? That face, that body, no way, I think my mouth watered I can't be sure but I know for damn sure every sense I ever had headed south.
"Hello Samantha." I kept my hands in my pockets, the girl's father was in the room after all it wouldn't do to throw her on the floor and ravish her the way I wanted to. What the hell happened to my self-control? She's a kid for crying out loud, and your dead friend's baby sister you perv. Yeah remember him? Your good buddy, I don't think he had this in mind when he asked you to

make that promise. Hands off. I think I heard my dick whine.

She cocked her head to the side, hands on her hips and those big blue grey eyes staring me down.

"Do I know you?"

"Sam!" Charlie sighed and shook his head.

"What dad? I'm just asking a question. So what the hell are you selling anyway, whatever it is..."

"Yes I heard, you don't need it, are you always this rude to your guests young lady?" She raised her head a notch.

"Since when are scum sucking salesmen guests?"

"Lord give us strength." Charlie closed his eyes as if in silent prayer.

"Gabriel Sweeney meet Annie Oakley."

"Very funny dad, so who are you now?"

"He was your brother's buddy in the army."

And just like that her whole persona changed, her body deflated slightly and there was a slight tightening of her mouth, and a glistening sheen formed in her eyes. She obviously still felt the loss of her brother deeply. Good now maybe you can get back on track.

"Phil talked about you constantly." I gave her a reassuring smile.

"Phillip." It was a heartfelt whisper; why did I have the uncontrollable urge to wrap her in my arms and shield her from all future hurts? She seemed to collect herself rather quickly though, it was to be admired.
"Okay well Phil's not here he's dead."

"For the love of... Samantha what is wrong with you?"
"Uh pop news flash, Phil's been gone for six years, why would one of his buddies be showing up here now? If he was a buddy then he would know he's dead, you're so gullible pop." With that she headed towards what I assume was the kitchen in the back of the house.
"Don't even think about it, get back in here."
She returned with a shotgun pointed right at me.

"Okay slick you got ten seconds two are up, who are you and what the hell do you want?"
Okay it was official she owned my dick. Did she have any idea how hot she was right now? If she ran off all unwanted guests like this it was a wonder some man hadn't snatched her up already. I felt anger and unfamiliar jealousy rise inside me

at the thought, no one better have laid a hand on her.

That totally came from a place of guardianship, not because I wanted to be the only man to put hands on her. Yeah right, keep telling yourself that Sweeney.

SAM

My heart was beating so fast I was in danger of passing out. He was so hot I felt like fanning myself, but I couldn't let him see that. Of course I knew who he was, as soon as I heard the name the face clicked. I had an old dog eared picture of a younger him up in my dresser, I'd had plenty of unSam like thoughts about him during my younger impressionable years, okay still did sometimes but not as much, well okay maybe...whatever. What I wanted to know was what was he doing here now. It had been six long years why would he be here now? And why was he looking at me like that, did I have something on my face or something?

I could swear he was fighting a smile while I pointed my gun at his head, was he too stupid to understand danger? Maybe that coma that he'd been in all those years ago had addled his brain. Bless his heart.

Pop was back to grumbling, but he didn't understand, this was my shield, my protection. If I didn't do this I would probably sit on the couch and simper at him like that stupid cow Diana Thorpe did with Dan Young, it was sickening.

"Samantha Eliza Holder..." Pop was three naming me again but I'll deal with that later; for now I just gave him a look, to which he glared back at me.

"Would you put that damn thing down and offer our guest something to drink."

I kissed my teeth and headed back to the kitchen glad for the reprieve, my legs were ready to give out so I sat down at the table. Well genius what's your next plan of action? I bit my nails as I contemplated my next move. I got up and opened the fridge, there was nothing but beer and soda in there and since I didn't know if Mr. Fancy drank domestic I went with a soda.

Returning to the room I called a heads up and threw the can at him, to which pop proceeded to have a conniption.

"What did I do to deserve this? Tell me, you took my legs and I took it the best I could, but did you have to send me one of Satan's imps to put me in an early grave?" Pop was having one of his many daily asides with our maker.

Meanwhile Mr. Cool caught and opened his can in one smooth move.

"It's okay sir, I think I'm kinda getting use to Samantha's antics." Oh you thought so did you? We'll just have to see about that, they didn't call me the hellion of Lexington for nothing. I wonder how long he was staying in these parts? I'd show him antics.

Chapter 4

Chief

I kept a stern face on but inside I was snickering, who did these two think they were fooling? I might've lost the use of my legs but the old noggin still worked very well thank you. I'd been a cop and a damn good one, I knew how to read people. There were more sparks flying off these two than a welder's flame, I guess my boy was right after all. Phillip had had some hair brained idea that these two would be perfect for each other, mind you when he first mentioned it I thought he'd lost his ever loving mind after all his sister was a child of twelve and Gabriel was already a grown man, but Phil had insisted that he knew what he knew and since the boy had always had a bit of the fey in him I let it be, after all who am I to stand in the way of destiny?

Right now Samantha was sneaking looks at our guest out the side of her eye, it was a wonder she didn't go cross eyed, meanwhile he was trying his best to play it cool but I knew for damn sure if I wasn't in the room he would've probably kissed her already. Either that or throttled her, the damn girl was a handful. Well, if nothing else it was sure going to be hopping around here for the next little while. If I knew anything about my daughter it was that there was never a dull moment. Lord knows what she would come up with to torture the poor man.

"So Gabriel you're staying with us of course." I broke the silence.

My dainty little flower huffed and snorted at the same time, I kid you not you had to see it to believe it. I didn't even look in her direction if I did I was sure she would be spitting fire at me with her eyes.

Delilah Spelman AKA Miss. Marple

Well, looks like no show for me today that young man's been over to Charlie's going on a good half hour and nothing, not a peep, unless Samantha killed him and buried him in the backyard. Lord I hope Charlie was home and not out gallivanting with that Geoffrey Godwin, those two still thinks they're teenagers with their beer swilling and caterwauling sometimes at all hours of the night. No wonder Samantha was such a hooligan, between her father and her Godfather she sure was getting an education.
Well I might as well head on inside, this infernal rain was starting to come down again, I could always stay close to the window just in case.

SAM

Now why would pop go and do such a stupid thing as to invite him to stay here? And who pray tell was supposed to look after him, huh?

"Pop"

"Sam."

I gritted my teeth he still wasn't looking at me.

"Maybe Mr. Sweeney has other plans."

"What other plans he can't be planning to head back all that way after only a short visit and there's no hotel in Lexington, use your common sense girl." At least he didn't use his usual refrain of " You don't have the good sense that God gave a duck".

"That's no trouble Charlie I was thinking of heading back to Annandale to find a hotel for the rest of my stay."

"Boy that's more than two hours back and forth nonsense, you'll stay here and that's final, Miss. Priss will make up Phil's old room it'll be fine."

I wondered what was the penalty for patricide in the good state of New York, and if that damn Gabriel didn't stop his snickering I was really going to lose it. Maybe I should put a little surprise in his bed, let him see how welcomed he was. Very mature Sam and damn if he wasn't looking at me like he expected just that. I turned my glare on him instead to let him see just what I thought of this state of affairs.

GABE

If looks could kill I'd be road kill.

Chapter 5

GABE

After spending the afternoon reminiscing with Charlie about Phil's childhood and being entertained by Samantha's antics it was time for dinner.

Between huffing and puffing her way throughout the house while muttering what I was sure were curse words under her breath, she'd been in the kitchen concocting something that smelled amazing.

Charlie pretty much ignored her while I couldn't keep my attention off of her, which I hoped he didn't notice. I was aware of her every move, she was like some kind of magnet, and she was so damn cute when she was pissed. I'm sure the chief would be getting an earful at her first convenience.

"So what do you think of our little Sam?" Shit, trick question how was I supposed to answer that? Obviously I couldn't tell him the truth that

I'd like to lay his daughter down on the nearest flat surface, spread her out and feast for the next few days. Way to go, now you have another boner to hide, shit.

"Uh, she's... Different?"

He almost choked on his beer, yes, we'd graduated to beer at some point.

"That's a very polite way of saying it son."

He snickered and I laughed.

"If you two hyenas are finished cackling dinner's on the table." She flounced in and out of the room, which just made us laugh even harder. We both stopped when we heard the ominous sound of the garbage disposal getting started. We made a speedy beeline for the kitchen Charlie beating me out by a nose.

"Come on Gabriel, it wouldn't be the first time I lost my dinner to her temper and I'm too lit to drive to the diner and so are you."

He was right about that, but would she really throw out dinner after working so hard to prepare it? Apparently so, since we found her in the kitchen standing over the sink with a plate in hand ready to do just that. "

"Sam, honey put the plate down, don't make your old man have go out in this rain to get something to eat." He looked so forlorn I wanted to laugh.

"Okay what did we do to set you off?"

"Nothing, you didn't do anything to set me off, whatever could you mean, it's just that you took so long to come when I called I figured you two weren't hungry." Butter wouldn't melt in her mouth, what a little spitfire, she said it all with a saccharin smile.

"Sorry about that hon, won't happen again, right Gabe boy?" I hated being called that but I could put up with it this once if it would placate her.

"Sure thing chief, my apologies Miss. Sam." She rolled her eyes at me and brought the plate back to the table. Figures it was mine. She glared at me when I thanked her then dropped down in the chair across from me.

"Such a lady my little princess is." Charlie teased as she glared at him. He must want to go hungry, I for one was suddenly starving so I kept my trap shut. That still didn't save me though. "Just so you know you can wash your own plate when you're done, I'm not the maid."

"Lord love a duck, Samantha Eliza Holder did you fall and hit your head? Where are your manners? Please excuse her Gabriel and don't worry about the dishes Miss. Manners over here does them."
"Not tonight she doesn't I have a date."
There were two very surprised men gaping at her, and what did she do after dropping that bombshell? The exasperating woman child proceeded to pick up her fork and eat as if she hadn't just thrown my world off its axis. Over my dead body she had a date. Fuck that.

Chapter 6

Chief

Oh shit Sam's done stirred up the hornets' nest; I know my little girl's innocent of the ways of men, so she didn't know the telltale signs of a man on the scent. I better head this off before things get ugly.

"A date, really Sam! Since when is pool with Brandon and the boys a date? Brandon's like a brother to her, they grew up together you know. His father's her Godfather and I'm his, he's family."

I hurried to explain to the young man who looked like he was about to explode at my table. Of course my contrary daughter wouldn't thank me for my interference seeing as how she was shooting daggers at me again with her eyes, but it was all for her benefit, she'd thank me one day, if she didn't brain me first, Lord where did I go wrong? She was such a quiet baby.

"Anyway I don't think you should play tonight,

we have guest, come on Sam one night isn't going to hurt anything, besides it wouldn't be polite." I gave her my most innocent look. Hah.

"I'm going." Oh Lord, crossed arms and the unibrow not a good combo, that meant she was working up a good head of steam. What to do, what to do.
"That's okay chief, I'm sure I can find something around here to keep me occupied."
I was a terrible father but I had to do it.
"Oh I know, I could call up that Diana Thorpe, or that Paula Winters and have one or the other show you around , they're Sam's girlfriends, I'm sure they wouldn't mind. Yes that would be perfect, that way Sam you won't have to miss your night out with your friends and poor Gabriel here wouldn't be stuck in this house bored out of his gourd. I go to sleep early son, wouldn't be any company at all." Not really but tonight I would be. I sat back and waited for the fire works to start.

SAM

"Pop...you...Di...Paul...arrrrrrgh." Was it possible to see red, I mean I've heard people say it before but this was the first time I'd actually experienced it myself. If either one of those hussies came within two feet of my Gabriel...oi, my Gabriel, since when? I felt my face heat up. Pop could be so infuriating sometimes.
"They're both busy tonight so you can't." I didn't know if that was true or not but over my dead body were they showing him around, they were both simpering ninnies and Paula was always on the prowl for a husband, I'm sure she'd take one look at Mr. Car and see dollar signs. I guess since he was my brother's long lost friend it was only right that I save him from her clutches.
"Says who, I'm sure either one of those beautiful young ladies would be more than happy to show our Gabriel around, maybe they can even drive up to the beaches at Ulster if it's not too late, it's very nice out there Gabriel."

The fool man just smiled and nodded like the village idiot, he had no idea what dad was suggesting subjecting him to, he'd shoot his own head off if he had to endure any amount of time with either of those cows. Bless his heart.

"Fine pop, I'll call Brand and cancel, happy now?"

"You don't have to change your plans on my account, I'll be perfectly happy with either this Diana or Paula person. "

I gave him a look that would strip paint.

"Shut it." He held up his hands in surrender and grinned at me like he knew a secret that I didn't.

GABE

Well, well, well, I think my little flower is jealous, interesting, very interesting indeed. I think I just might call home and make arrangements to extend my stay. I haven't had a real vacation in years I had a team of executives that could more than hold their own for a while. I looked away in time to catch that gleam in Charlie's eyes again. Yes indeed things were going to be interesting around here.

Chapter 7

GABE

Dinner was...interesting to say the least, the food I have to say was superb but the company was...interesting. Charlie tried his best to keep the conversation going, but the other occupant was either huffing or rolling her eyes.
"Was there something else you wanted to discuss besides sports Samantha?" Too late I saw Charlie shaking his head in warning out the side of my eye but when I turned around he was suddenly very interested in some imaginary spot on the ceiling.
Our delightful little Miss. Sunshine huffed at me again before lighting into us, or should I say all men everywhere?
"Yes actually I would, since I don't see the big deal about a bunch of grown men running around with pigskin in their hands while trying to knock the sense the good Lord gave them out of each other's heads, or that other insipid game where

grown men stand around waiting to catch a ball that could knock their stupid teeth out of their fat stupid heads while another fool stands around waiting to hit it, and don't get me started on golf, I mean what the H E double hockey sticks?"
You'd think she was done, not by a long shot.

"Meanwhile these jerks are making millions while the men and women responsible for teaching your children get diddly squat. Now you tell me Mr. Big shot in what universe is that even remotely acceptable? Men."
Oh boy better not introduce her to Jon anytime soon.
Charlie made as if to speak but was cut off.
"And what about those goons on ice? A perfect example of bullying gone way wrong: and what is with you men and balls anyway? Every game has to be centered around balls, I don't know seems kinda telling to me." And with that she folded her arms and the show was over. Charlie was once again inspecting the ceiling, which meant I was on my own.

"Okay then Samantha what would you like to talk about."
"Must you say my name like that?"

"Uh, excuse me, like what?"

"Well okay Samantha." She snarked at me, no seriously with high falsetto accent and all, I would've been offended if she wasn't do damn cute. There was a car door closing in the driveway which thank heavens provided me with a reprieve.

"Oh shoot, I forgot to call Brandon."

"Sammy poo where are ya, you ready?"

A man entered the kitchen, kind of built, stocky, not quite six feet tall, heavy on the Native American, and made a beeline for my Sam. He picked her up from her chair and twirled her around while she laughed like a little girl it was the most carefree I'd seen her since I'd been here and it was for another man, a man who had his hands on her...

I saw Charlie once again sizing me up out of the corner of my eye, what I wanted to know was why wasn't he telling this big gorilla to unhand his daughter? No brotherly type would have his hand on her ass. Fuck no, I was ready to tear him from limb to limb but Charlie apparently woke up out of his stupor in time to save the kid from an ass whipping.

"Brand put the girl down we got company."
"Oh hey man I didn't see you there. Brandon
Godwin, friends call me Brand."
"Brandon." You aren't really contemplating
having a pissing contest with a kid are you
Sweeney? I politely shook his hand, barely
restraining myself from crushing the bones in his.
"Gabriel Sweeney."
"Yeah man pleased to meet ya, so come on Sam
you ready?"

I folded my arms across my chest like an
ADD kid about to throw the mother of all
tantrums. If she even thought of stepping out that
door with him, I couldn't be held responsible for
my actions. Brother my ass, were these two blind?
It was plain as the nose on his face that he wanted
her, too fucking bad buddy she was off the market
as of ten o'clock this morning, run along now, go
play with your other friends because if I had my
way the last time she went anywhere alone with
you, was the last time she went anywhere alone
with you.
"Uhm, Brand Bear I was gonna call you, I can't
go, you know guest and all." She pointed at me
like an afterthought. Oh really. And what the hell

was up with that Brand Bear shit. God now I'm snarking.

"Aw come on Sammy Charlie's here he can keep him company, besides he's Charlie's guest right."

"Brandon why don't you head on out with your friends? Sam will see you next week alright." Charlie had the good sense to pipe in. The kid looked like he wanted to argue but then thought better of it.

"Walk me out Sam." He practically dragged her out of the room and it took everything I had not to follow them and break his damn arm, he better keep his hands to himself if he knew what was good for him. I started counting down the seconds. Shit I'd met her less than twelve hours ago and already she'd made me insane.

Chief

Man I'm getting too old for this shit; I could swear Brandon just came to within an inch of losing his life. If I were into theatrics I would wipe the imaginary sweat off my brow. Another bloodshed averted, then again it was only eight in the evening who knows what my delightful daughter would get up to between now and midnight?

If she didn't get back in here soon I was afraid Gabriel would go out there and drag her back and then the sparks would really start to fly. I wish she would hurry up cause I couldn't get between two hulking men if it came to that.

SAM

"Brandon what the heck has gotten into you and what was that in the kitchen? Next time you touch my butt I'll break your nose."
"Calm down sassyfrass I just didn't like the way that guy was looking at you."
"Looking at me, how was he looking."
"Like he owned you." Oh wow why that make me feel all tingly inside!
"Don't be silly Brand he's Phil's old war buddy that's all."
"Sure Sammy boo." He ruffled my hair before heading out the door.
Brandon had to be wrong, there's no way fancy car was looking at me like that; that didn't stop me from getting the tingles again though. Okay Sam game face on, you have a guest to terrorize.

Chapter 8

SAM

Okay so I know most people think I'm difficult, but I'm not really, I'm just...different, I'm not a girly girl and I'm not a tomboy either, I'm kind of a cross in between. I like some girly things but I was never going to be a simpering ninny, but what Brandon said made me feel like giggling and all of a sudden I had butterflies in my tummy and my body felt hot for some strange reason. Of course I was blushing, what else is new?

Dad and Gabriel were having coffee by the time I returned to the kitchen.

"Sam how come you don't have pie? I could've sworn I smelled pie."

"Whining in the elderly is so unattractive." I went to get the pie from the rack where it was cooling in plain sight of both Neanderthals, I turned to give them a glare, what, they couldn't get their own pie?

"Watch who you're calling elderly and I wasn't whining I was simply asking a question." Of course he was whining again.
"Do you want pie as well Gabriel?" Why the hell was I blushing? Stupid Brandon and his stupid thoughts.
"I'd love some."

Somebody had cleared the table and I was almost certain it wasn't dad.
"Thank you for clearing the dishes."
"Hey, I could've been the one who did that, how come you only thank him?"
"Because whiny whining stein, you're three quarters useless in the kitchen."
"See Gabriel this is the thanks I get after all my hard work too." I snorted at him, my dad was a caveman, women did female things and men did manly things and ne'er the twain should meet. He didn't let his being in the chair stop him from doing anything either, he did what needed to be done even if it took him twice as long as everyone else, that's my dad, he's my hero.

GABE

She came back in eight minutes, as she joked around with her father I noticed a slight flush on her cheeks and it pissed me the fuck off, if she'd let that boy kiss her I would ring her pretty little neck. I was so damn furious it was a wonder steam wasn't coming out of my ears. When she asked me about pie I was hard pressed to answer in a civilized manner, we were going to have to have a conversation pretty damn soon. It didn't matter that we'd just met or that she was my deceased buddy's sister, not even the nine years difference in our age mattered to me, I wanted her, what I want I take, plain and simple. I wondered how shocked she was going to be when I laid down the law, knowing my little angel she'll be spitting nails and threatening me with a gun no doubt, too bad. I had her in my cross hairs now, it was over for her, if she gave me too much trouble I could always turn her over my knee, seems to me Charlie had been a bit lax in the disciplinary department.

I watched her beautiful round ass as she walked back and forth getting pie for her father and I, that hair alone was enough to bring me to my knees, it was wild and untamed just like its' owner, tumbling all the way down her back to her ass in a fiery red that foretold of the temper that was so rumored to come with it; I 'd enjoy wrapping it around...what the fuck? Where the hell did I just go in my head? No woman had ever captivated me like this before, and definitely not at first meeting. Yes I've found women attractive in the past but I usually have more self control than this, those newspapers that liked to talk about my playboy bachelor status would laugh their asses off if they could see me now, brought low by a mere girl. I gritted my teeth and fought against the rising of the south. I 've been in a perpetual state of horny since I first saw her, I hope to God Charlie didn't catch on to my thoughts before I had a chance to talk to him. Speaking of which...

I turned to the man in question sure that he'd just caught me ogling his daughter's ass.

"We need to talk."

Chief

Yes indeed things were heating up around here, Gabriel was chomping at the bit, Miss. Priss was blushing fire engine red and her insults were a little tamer than usual which meant she was flustered, now if I didn't know better I would think it was Brandon's doing, but I did know better, Brandon hadn't put that look on my little girls' face, plus she kept taking peaks at Gabriel when she thought no one was looking.
I of course pretended not to be paying attention to either of them but nothing got by me. Now if I could just keep her from killing him and vice versa maybe we could have us a wedding in the near future. My Sam was young in years yes, but she was old in spirit and she needed to settle down quick, and preferably with some one that could rein her in before she ended up on America's Most Wanted.

She dropped the pie in front of us just as Gabriel was demanding to talk to me. I wonder what he could need to talk about. Yes indeed

Brandon had stirred up the hornet's nest. I'll have to talk to the boy about where he put his hand the next time we met though. Or I'm sure Gabriel would help him off with it. These young people are so quick to get fired up.

"Whenever you wanna talk son I'm here." Lord if there's gonna be some type of courtship please let me survive it. I looked up in prayer.

"What're you bothering God about now dad?"

"Nothing honey bear, nothing at all. " I got the huff, the eye roll and the unibrow altogether.

Chapter 9

GABE

When Sam went for her evening bath I figured it was as good a time as any to talk to Charlie so we met in the living room.

"What's on your mind son?"

"Well sir, this is going to sound all kinds of weird since we just met but uh, I uhmm." Shit this was harder than I thought.

"Just spit it out son."

Okay here goes. "I want to date your daughter, in fact I'm pretty sure it's more than that but we'll start there for now." There, I'd said it.

He was looking rather contemplative as if he had to give it some thought, which was understandable, after all he didn't know me from Adam, but he trusted Phil's judgment so I had that working for me.

"Well son she's of age, just turned eighteen so I can't rightly tell her what to do."

"Understood, but is it okay with you, I am older than her by a few years and let's face it all you know about me is what your twenty year old son told you seven years ago." He waved off that suggestion.

"Son I've been reading people all my life, even did it for a living, if I didn't trust you I would've let Annie Oakley shoot you this morning."

"So I have your blessing then?"

"Sure do son let's shake on it." We shook hands and I sat back on the couch.

"Well from what I can see she's going to be a handful I'm going to need all the help I can get."

"No sir you're on your own."

Say what now! I looked at him in disbelief and he looked back at me serious as a judge.

"It's simple son, you want her, you figure it out, me, I like having supper on the table and clean sheets on my bed, I'm not getting involved in your hullabaloo and I'd thank you to apprise her of that fact, which means if you screw up it's all on you, not me, and trust me son, you will screw up, that's a given, that one up those stairs is as ornery as a disturbed rattler. I'd walk softly if I was you, and you might want to look into getting a big stick." He had the nerve to shake his head in consternation. Okay then I could do this, I have dated before and I had quite a few years experience. I'm sure Sam had very little if any at all she better fucking not have any. Yeah that's fair. I didn't give two shits about being fair if she did have any it was all in the past, her only experiences were going to be with me from now on.

Chief

I wonder what has him scowling now? He seems to be just as contrary as Samantha, Lord what a pair. Well, the die was cast; let's see where the chips fell, if nothing else it sure was going to be interesting. I watched the two of them circling around each other all day sniffing out their territory my boy was right all along he knew what he knew, made for each other, yes indeed.
Now all I had to do was lock up all sharp objects and firearms the first time he said no to her about something, that girl did like her way. I hoped to God I survived this courtship. I wonder if Geoffrey was up for a week -long fishing trip? No better not, somebody had to be here to bury the bodies. I need a drink.

Chapter 10

GABE

My first night at the Holder residence was...interesting. After my shower I headed back downstairs to say goodnight to the chief since his room was located on the first floor for obvious reasons.

I walked in on father and daughter having their nightly ritual it looked like. The little she cat with the sharp claws was gone in her place was a little lamb who sat on the floor at her father's feet with her head on his knees while he played with her hair and whispered to her. I didn't quite catch what was being said but I could tell by the ease with which they interacted that this was nothing new. It was heartwarming to see.

I snuck back up the stairs not wanting to intrude on their moment, but with a new hope for the future. It seemed my Sam had a soft side. It wouldn't be all shotguns and tirades. One thing was for sure; my life would never be dull with her in it.

The next day started with a bang. I was halfway down the stairs when I heard the racket.

"Why can't I have French toast?"

"Because I already made the batter for my special pancakes."

"But I want French toast."

"How about bread and water? One more word about the stupid French toast, just one more."

To which Charlie started grumbling under his breath.

I entered the kitchen tentatively to say the least.

"Good morning... Sam." Charlie was making slashing motions across his throat and shaking his head vigorously.

"What's so good about it huh?" she banged a pot down on the stovetop.

Oookay then the she cat was back in full force it looked like.

Charlie mouthed the word coffee and something else I didn't catch and rolled his eyes. I was a bit confused until he pointed to Sam, behind her back of course and then the coffee pot, I noticed the coffee was now finishing up. Ah, I get it; she hasn't had her first cup yet. Good to know.

I took a seat across from Charlie as the princess of the castle bustled around making what looked like apple pancakes.

" How was your night son, sleep okay?" He questioned me while keeping a weary eye on his offspring.

"Everything was just great Charlie thanks."

There was more grumbling coming from Sam's side. He leaned over and whispered to me.

"Don't say anything to set her off or we'll both be wearing pancake batter."

"What's that dad?" He rolled his eyes behind her back.

"Oh nothing precious, I was just telling Gabriel here that we'll be having dinner at the Lodge tonight."

Really, that was news to me; I tried not to laugh at the look of apprehension on his face. These two should take this act on the road. Charlie and I passed the time making small talk and trying not to piss off my little flower while we waited for breakfast, I don't think Charlie drew a breath until she placed his plate in front of him. Then she kissed his head like nothing happened,

like she hadn't just been griping at him. I hope I
was up to the task of dealing with all her moods.
I'm sure I'll have a few grey hairs before too long.
She was looking very pretty this morning in a blue
pullover and a denim skirt, her long hair flowing
freely. Every time our eyes met she would blush
in the prettiest way and lower her head, I didn't
even know women still did that.
I enjoyed my breakfast, which again was nothing
short of amazing and waited to see what the day
will hold. It was bound to be entertaining.

Chapter 11

GABE

I spent the day with my Sam and It was ...enlightening. Charlie browbeat her into showing me around their little town later in the afternoon. We walked the entire thing in less than half an hour; it literally consisted of the school, which catered to kindergarten through twelfth grade. The diner the Lodge where the billiard hall was located and a grocery store. There were some other little Knick knack type places but nothing major.

It was kind of quaint though, and would've been nice except for the rain, it was cloudy when we left and seemed to stay that way. In fact it had been either cloudy or raining since I arrived.

It was quite an education to watch how the locals reacted to Samantha. The older men treated her like one of their grand kids, if only with a little subtle flirting thrown in for good measure, which seemed to go right over my flowers' head.

The older women seemed a little disapproving if not leery, but still with a touch of indulgence, while the young men Sam's age all seemed taken with her. Especially some kid called Young, bastard had the nerve to ogle her right in front of me, of course I had to stake my claim, so I took my life and my nuts in my hands and dropped my arm across her shoulders while glaring at the kid with the death wish. He got the message and luckily for me she didn't snap my arm or my head off, just gave me a strange look. We suspiciously didn't run into any of her female friends.

When we left the Young kid and headed home she finally let me know what she thought of my little stunt.

"Next time why don't you pee on me?"
"Excuse me?" Color me confused.
"What was that back there If not some macho nonsense? I'm not a meaty bone you know."
She folded her arms and huffed.
" I didn't realize that's what I was doing." I lied through my teeth, so sue me.
"Sure you didn't." And there we have the eye roll.
"Like I said, next time just raise your leg and let

fly, then they'd know you've marked your territory. Just be careful that I'm not armed with any sharp objects before you do it, snip, snip." She had the nerve to laugh; I think I felt my balls draw up in fear with a little pitiful whine.

Geez she was unbelievable, to see her she was all innocence and sweet, not exactly girl next door no, that wild hair and those fuck me lips didn't scream girl next door, they screamed hot sex and raunchy delights. Damn I needed to calm down my thoughts around her. My balls were going to change color soon.
We walked the rest of the way in relative silence, while giving each other surreptitious looks when we each thought the other wasn't looking.
"Well hey there Samantha, who's your new young man?"
The voice came from across the street from Charlie's house, there was an elderly lady sitting on the porch with what looked like an old fashioned bourbon flask and some knitting paraphernalia rocking back and forth in a rocker. Sam of course started grumbling only God knows what under her breath, all I caught was "the nosy old bat." at which I coughed to hide the laugh that wanted to escape.

"Afternoon Miss. Spelman, this is Phil's friend from the army." She introduced me to the lady who eyed me up and down, sizing me up as though measuring my worth.

" Saw him pull up yesterday didn't I, so how long you staying young man?" She squinted at me; I'm thinking that flask didn't hold afternoon tea.

Sam started shuffling her feet as though she was in a hurry.

"Well ma'am I'm thinking maybe a week or two...for now."

"Seen something you like did you?" She gave me a telling look which I ignored and had her cackling.

I hadn't quite gotten around to telling Sam about my newfound interest in her and she didn't need to find out in front of what I was almost sure was the neighborhood gossip.

"We have to get going Miss. Spelman, dad's waiting for us, see you later. I'll be sure to bring you that blueberry pie for the church social."

'That's lovely dear, I hope you'll still have time what with all the goings on." Whatever else she had to say was lost on us as Sam practically dragged me across the street.

"Slow down there love." I pulled back on her hand gently to slow her progress.

"Try to keep up gramps; we have to get lost before she thinks up anymore nosy questions. We'll be out here till kingdom come if she has her way."

My girl sure could do a snit with the best of them, didn't take much to set her off on one of her tangents either.

"Sam, I wanted to talk to you about something important."

She looked up at me a touch warily.

"Sure I guess."

"Let's sit here on the porch." I drew her down on the swing and sat down beside her, still holding her hand. Either she didn't notice or she didn't mind too much. I was hoping for the latter.

"I spoke to your father about us dating." No sense in beating around the bush, besides she wouldn't appreciate it I was sure.

She tensed up for a split second before relaxing. Then I thought I actually saw steam come out of her ears. I found myself bracing for whatever was coming next but I was ready for her every argument. My one strength was that there was no sense in pretending that I wasn't interested; she struck me as the type who would appreciate honesty and though this was rather sudden I saw no point in putting it off. Not to mention the fact that in a town this size she was sure to be snatched up sooner or later unless the men in this place were blind or stupid. How the hell she'd evaded being claimed by some man or bot before now looking the way she did I'd never know, then again that temper of hers had probably turned away more than her fair share of admirers. Funnily enough I wanted the whole package all that fire wrapped up in that beautiful package it was enough to make me salivate like a green boy with his first crush.

"What do you mean you spoke to my father about dating me, shouldn't you have asked me first?"
Oh shit. "Well, proper etiquette demands that I speak with him first, get his approval."
"Well excuse me for living in the twenty first century. " She tried to pull her hand away but I held fast.
"What if I'm not interested? I'm not chattel you know, you and my father just can't decide that I'm going to date you."
"Don't you want to?" I was going out on a limb

here, she could totally shoot me down but somehow I didn't think so. There was no way what I felt was one sided, fate wouldn't be that cruel.

Of course fate might not be, but my flower was a prickly cactus half the time, who knew which way the wind would blow? She'd only laid eyes on me in the flesh for the first time a day ago and not everyone was as gungho as me, she could be a cautious type under all that fire and passion not that it was going to make a bit of difference I the long run, not after I've seen her and wanted her.
I noticed she was having a hard time answering me but she was blushing in that becoming way that I was growing to love, instead of pushing my luck I made a suggestion that was sure to meet with her approval.

"Hey!" I lifted her chin with my finger, it was the first time I'd touched her like this and I was hard pressed not to kiss her, she felt so soft. I had to shake my head to clear it, damn I felt like a green boy next to her.
"Why don't we try it and see how you like it, if you're not comfortable then we'll chalk it up to

experience. What do you say?" Like hell.
She took her sweet time answering making me sweat, there was no doubt in my mind that this was going to happen but it would be so much better not to mention safer for yours truly if she was on board. I didn't fancy having to hogtie her and spirit her away which was always an option granted I could get chief to go along with it.

"Well as long as you don't expect me to sit around making goo goo eyes at you and simpering all day, cause I've got better things to do," I started to ask her what the hell she was talking about but apparently she wasn't finished.
"And I'm not wearing skirts up to my navel so everyone could see what I had for breakfast, or those death traps that look like you're walking on stilts."

Okay, she's talking about short skirts and high heels...I think.
"And don't even think that I'm putting a pound of gook on my face to look pretty for you, you'll take me as I am or you can go back to Virginia and find a mannequin to play dress up."
I kept my mouth shut and let her finish her rant;

she had a lot to say after she got started.
I learned something sitting on that porch, two
things really. My flower didn't know the first
thing about dating, it was going to be up to me to
guide her, I was looking forward to it, and second,
she ranted like a mad person when she was
nervous.

GABRIEL'S PROMISE | 63

Chief

I'm sitting here in the living room, now mind you I didn't mean to eavesdrop; I was just taking a much -needed breather in between Sam's moods. Lord knows what kind of mood she'd be in when they got back; but then I heard him tell her that he'd spoken to me when I could've sworn I told that boy to leave me out if it. Well...I'm sure I'll be hearing about it later, but now I have bigger fish to fry.

My Sam seems stuck in the seventeen hundreds, I had no idea the girl was so green. I guess that's what I get for letting the Bronte sisters raise her, the girl always had one of their novels attached to her nose.

Now the boy had the right of it, and I would've thought that my delightful Miss. Priss with her antiquated views would appreciate that. Of course being Sam, she could just be being contrary for the sake of being contrary. I rolled my eyes at the thought of both of them.

I hope I'm not gonna have to get too involved in

this courtship nonsense, I had no time for it and Sam is a handful to begin with, you add hormones and affairs of the heart into the mix and I'd have a minefield on my hands.

Lord I should've sent that boy packing the first day he showed up here. Good Lord was that only yesterday? Seems like so long ago; well that's life with Sam for ya, never a dull moment. Deep, deep sigh.

Chapter 12

SAM

Way to sound like a hayseed Sam geez, why can't you ever shut up? Yes I 'm talking to myself I have some of my best conversations this way, seeing as how most people are dumber than a bag of rocks.

I can't wait to get my hands on one Chief Holder, he practically gave me away and didn't even bother to say word one to me about it, well we'll just see about that.

I know I'm rambling, but what do you expect? Mr. Fancy car is interested in dating me, what the h e double hockey sticks am I suppose to do? Who can I ask for advice? I can't ask Charlie since I'm not speaking to him ever again in this millennium, those two vapid waste of space are out, and Brand's a boy he would be no help, but it would sure be good to have someone to tell me what I'm supposed to do. My friend Mandy might've been of some help but she's gone for the summer. Maybe I can watch a movie about it, I'll have to check. Not now though, because it's time to get ready for the lodge.

Going through my stupid closet all I see are jeans and tees, or sweaters, nothing fancy, I never needed anything fancy to go to the lodge before. Way in the back I found this yellow dress that Mandy got me for my birthday, I never wore it because it made me look like a canary. Bright yellow really, what am I big bird?
Well I'm not driving myself crazy it's jeans and...something and that's that.

Chief

Well...Miss. Priss came through the door
after their little talk, took one look at me and stuck
her nose in the air.
Oh boy, I know what that means, doghouse, and
not just any doghouse, this one was made for a
mastiff.
I gulped nervously, only heaven knows what she
has in store for me, I know one thing, it won't be
good. She's been up in her room for the past few
hours, either trying to get ready for her pseudo
first date, Lord knows that could be a disaster of
monumental proportions Carrie Bradshaw my girl
isn't or plotting my demise.
What, you don't think I saw S.I.T.C? I live in
small town New York not outer Crimea, the only
person who hasn't seen it is my little gingersnap
because according to her it's all sniveling tripe.
Anyway either she's up there trying to outfit
herself, or she's building something illegal that
goes boom, for which I will be blamed because
it's always the parent's fault.

"Sam sweetheart it's almost time, you ready?" Deathly silence, I looked at Don Juan de Mariner who just came down the stairs decked out like he was headed to the Ritz.
"Son where the blazes are you going?" He looked around all kinds of confused.
"I thought we were going to the lodge."
"The lodge yes, the lodge is old jeans and flannels son, not dress slacks and button down shirts." I had to roll my eyes, I mean am I gonna have to teach these two everything?

"Sorry chief but I didn't pack anything like that, maybe next time." He had the nerve to clap me on the shoulder in what I believe was a condescending way; young people, they think they know everything.
Speaking of which, time to give Naomi Campbell another nudge, yes I know, two different ethnicities but the same personality if you get my drift.

"Sugar blossoms." That's my trick for softening her up whenever she gets mad at me, not that it ever works, that child hasn't been soft since the age of three.
A shoe or something, came flying down the stairs,

I guess that was my cue to leave well enough alone.

" This is all your fault." I fumed at big mouth beneath my breath.

"What's all my fault, what are you talking about?"

I had to whisper since I was in enough trouble already and if I wanted any peace in the next decade I had to tread carefully.

"I told you not to involve me didn't I? Couldn't you tell the girl you were interested without calling me into it? It's a real shame that you had to sell out an old man to make your life easier. Now she's all kinds of ticked off and who knows how long that will last, all I know is if she doesn't let me have my cobbler tonight I'm taking it out of your hide."

GABE

We were bickering in low voices back and forth when we heard her on the steps.
I think my boy stood up and did the happy dance, she looked amazing; she was dressed in this yellows dress that came to her knees, it had thin straps and belled out when she walked. The top had some kind of gathering that molded her pert breast beautifully. Maybe she needed a shawl or something to cover up, couldn't have other guys looking at her and who knew who was going to be at this lodge.
The color did something to her light colored eyes, she'd left her hair free flowing with just some sort of sparkly clip holding up one side.

"Wow, Sam, you look ...lovely." I wanted to cuff the chief as I saw him rolling his eyes out the side of mine.
"Yeah, precious you look..."
"Shut it." Oops, she gave him the death glare, I guess he was right, she was mad at him, though for the life of me I couldn't figure out why.

She came fully down the stairs and I took her hand in mine which made her blush, which in turn made my dick hard. First chance I get I'm finding a sporting goods store I needed a protective cup to hide my constant condition around this girl. How was I suppose to get through tonight with her looking and smelling like that? And that innocent air about her, man, I'm a goner for sure.

Charlie for some unknown reason tried to run me over with his chair on the way to the door but I didn't spare him a second thought, I had eyes only for my flower who looked ready to be plucked.

Chapter 13

GABE

We took Charlie's truck to the lodge, I took in the passing scenery for what it was worth pretty much just the same places I'd seen on my walk but at least now unlike then I could actually concentrate on what I was looking at. The town square revolved around the local courthouse that for some reason reminded me of the Capitol building. People were out and about most of them sitting in front of a little store front mom and pop type ice cream parlor, maybe one day before I had to leave I'll take Samantha there for a cone.

When we arrived everyone in the place turned to watch our entry, most of them were at least a hundred years old but there were some younger people there as well.
I saw two blondes making a beeline for us and almost jumped out of my skin when I felt Sam take my hand. Of course their eyes zeroed in on that telling action.

"Hi Sam." She was right, they simpered, it hadn't taken me long to figure out who they were and her show of possession made my chest swell, maybe there was hope for me yet.

"Diana, Paula." By now she had a death grip on my arm but I'm not complaining, the chief seems to be coming down with some sort of coughing fit and I was about to ask if he was okay when my prickly pear kicked his chair none too gently. I hope she didn't hurt herself, those flat things on her feet didn't look like much protection.
Whatever, it put paid to his coughing fit.

They were both looking at me as though waiting for an introduction, when I realized Sam wasn't about to do the honors I took matters in hand.
"Hello ladies, I'm Gabriel." I tried to shake hands but Sam made it clear she was not letting go so it was a bit awkward.
Meanwhile the chief is rolling his eyes all over his head like he's having a seizure, what was with him? I can't say I didn't like Sam's little show of being territorial. It was funny and sweet at the

same time. She just never ceased to amaze me, her social graces were missing altogether but that didn't seem to matter to me, she was unique.

"We're going to eat now and don't you two find excuses to come hobnobbing over there we'll be stuffing our faces and won't have time for small talk, see ya." With that Lady Di steered us towards their usual table in the dining hall. She left those two poor girls standing there red faced, I didn't know if I should laugh or scold her.
The chief as usual was rolling his eyes at us.

"Miss. Priss you take the cake, you really do, it's a wonder I can hold my head up in this town with a harridan like you for a daughter." There didn't seem to be any heat to his words and she didn't seem to take offense other than to give him another death glare before declaring, "Shut it, before I tell Sheila your sugar's too high this week."
"Now why you wanna go and do some fool thing like that? You know she's worse than you...I mean, come on now my little bluebell you don't have to do that, I'll behave, you know how I look forward to the cobbler here." He gave her an innocent smile and I snorted, yeah like that was

going to work.

He hung his head and apologized or at least he tried to.

"I'm sorry for calling you a harridan you're the best daughter in the whole world, a real gem, a princess among women.

Maybe it would've worked if he hadn't been rolling his eyes the whole time he was spewing that drivel and I knew if I could see it so could flower, so in the end all he got for his effort was a "Shut it." and then she put the menu up to her face.

I'm thinking I might need to take the chief to the eye specialist and get him checked out, it can't be healthy to roll your eyes in that way as often as he did. Interesting as always.

Chapter 14

GABE

"So what's good here Samantha?" She still had ahold of my arm and I wondered if she realized she still did until I noticed her staring daggers at someone or something across the room. When I followed her glare I found Diana and Paula on the receiving end, with their heads together whispering as their eyes remained glued to yours truly. Uh oh, my girl was not a happy camper.

"Sam would you unhand the poor man? He's not gonna run away, no need to get all clingy already."

She ignored him and kept her eyes pealed on her quarry. I had a hard time stifling my humor, who knew my little hellcat would be so territorial? I love it, since I felt pretty much the same way. She'd hooked me with one damn look wait until Jon heard about this he'll laugh his ass off.

When she finally relaxed her grip I took that to mean the stare down was over, so I repeated my question.

"So what's good here?" I took her hand under the table, which made her draw in her breath, which in turn alerted the chief that something was up, which he soon figured out because his daughter was blushing like a ripe cherry tomato. I rubbed my finger over her palm and acted as though it was the most natural thing in the world. She finally relaxed enough to answer my question.

"You'll have to ask the carnivore, I only ever get the vegetable lasagna or the mushroom ravioli." She pointed at the chief who muttered something about rabbit food under his breath. "And for your information pop, not that I'm talking to you, but for the sake of clarification..."

"Ooh, big words." He wriggled his eyebrows at her to which she snarled.

"The reason I was holding onto him is because if either one of those nitwits get their hooks into him the poor man would suffer a fate worse than death."

I was pretty sure that wasn't it but I held my tongue; I guess the chief felt the same way because he just huffed and looked at his menu. "The prime rib's the way to go son...I don't want to hear a peep out of you Dame Goodall, I like meat, most red blooded men do, I can't survive on grass and grains, I'm neither a cow, sheep nor goat.
"Are you calling me a goat?"

I thought it prudent to diffuse the situation before it became violent, so as the chief opened his mouth to reply I cut him off.
"What about fish?"
"Fish is fine, I like fish." She squeezed my hand.
"Fish is fine I like fish." He actually mocked her I guess he has a death wish. Sparks were coming out of her eyes, until the waitress came over with a jovial smile.

"Well hello Holders, and guest."
"Sheila this is Gabriel, Gabriel Sheila. The introductions were made and we shook hands. I saw my girl smile a real genuine smile for perhaps the first time since we met except for when that Brandon kid came over, I didn't like that one bit. "How's it going Sam, this one being good? She

tapped the chief who was unusually quiet on his shoulder. He was suddenly looking very uncomfortable.

"I wish Sheila, but you know how it is, he hasn't been taking his meds again, threw everything off and you know what doc said, when that happens we have to watch his food intake, so definitely no red meat, no sweets of any kind, and absolutely no caffeine." She shook her head, sober as a judge. Had I not known better I would've believed her.
The poor waitress was hanging on her every word, meanwhile, the chief beginning to look bilious, I don't think even Sam turned that shade when she blushed.

"Oh and no salt, for at least a week, so if he shows up here without me you be sure and see that he eats right. We want him with us for a long, long time."
He started sputtering all over his face, but neither female paid him the least bit of attention. I kept my trap shut in fear that she'd spoil my dinner as well. Though I was going to have the prime rib. I

couldn't have Samantha starting out on the wrong foot thinking she could dictate to me.

I ordered my meat with a fully loaded potato and ignored the rumblings coming from Sam. When Sheila told Charlie she had just the thing for him I thought he was going to cry. He looked like a little lost puppy.
Samantha meanwhile was beaming from ear to ear as happy as could be. What was I getting myself into? I did see a little of my old friend in her though, but she was her own unique brand of...something. Our kids were sure going to be something.
Say what now? Better leave that alone for now.

When Sheila brought out our food Sam literally bounced in her seat and clapped, at first I thought she was really excited about her vegetable lasagna, until the waitress placed a plate of steamed veggies in front of the chief, I kid you not, I think he whimpered. There had to be every green vegetable known to man on his plate. Broccoli, spinach, kale I think I even saw some zucchini on there for good measure. I would've laughed if it wasn't so mean. Then again he knew the risk, should've kept his mouth shut.
Of course he tried to get me in trouble by eyeing

my plate, but my tiger lily had that covered.
"Try it mister and this will be our one and only
date."
Needless to say the chief was on his own.

Chapter 15

GABE

I woke up this morning with new purpose. The cold war was in full force around here, now the chief wasn't talking to his daughter either and they were both so mature about it. The ride home had been an experience; it was like taking a cross country trip with three toddlers and a newborn for all that it was less than a ten minute drive from the Lodge to the house. This is how it went.

"Samantha Eliza Holder you're grounded." He griped as he maneuvered the truck out of the parking lot.
"Says who?"
"Says who? Says who? Says your father that's who."
"What are the grounds? " She sounded like a negotiator.
"I don't need any stinking grounds my word is law.
She snorted at that one.

"Sorry old man that's not a good enough argument try again."

He tried to get me in the middle with his next question but I was on to his tricks, he wasn't getting me thrown in the doghouse with him. "Do you see what I have to put up with? Ever since the age of three when she learned the English language instead of that gibberish she used to spout at me, she's done nothing but mouth off at me, now do you think that's right?" I held my hands up and became very interested in my surroundings. I think he cussed at me under his breath.
"I never spoke gibberish in my life you old coot." She was really enjoying egging him on.

"That's it you're grounded until you're twenty one."
"Shut it chief before I take the remote upstairs and hide it." Oh he almost came out of his seat at that one.
"You're no kid of mine, no kid of mine would ever be that mean, I got jipped at the hospital, somebody took my sweet little baby girl and sent

me home with Rosemary's baby."

Were these two for real? This shit had to be scripted.

"More like they sent innocent old me home with the Stepfather."

"Who, who's that, is that the crazy man that tried to kill his family?"

If I didn't get away from these two fast I was gonna piss myself, and holding in that much laughter for so long was starting to hurt.

They kept it up until we reached the driveway, it was starting to get dark but there was still some light left. The same lady was on her porch across the way again.

"Hey there chief, nice night ain't it?" She yelled across to us.

"Hey there Miss. Dee, how you doing? I should've known he was up to something when I saw the gleam in his eyes.

"We were just now talking about you my Sam was just saying how it's been a long time since she fixed up your hair. How long's it been now, it must be a good month or more."

"You know you're right, I hadn't thought of it, that's right nice of her you come on over

anytime you're ready Sam."
"She'll be there tomorrow." He grinned under his
breath; I of course had no idea what that was
about just now, but from the death rays coming
from flower's eyes it was not good.
"You vile decrepit old man, oh you are so gonna
pay for that."

"Am I missing something?" I didn't think
that question warranted harsh punishment,
apparently I was right because she answered me
without too much heat.
"I hate doing her hair, I hate going to her house
she has fifty cats and it smells like pee all the
time. Every time I come back from over there I
have to fumigate myself.
The chief had raced his chair up the ramp and into
the house no doubt to grab his precious remote
before she got her hands on it.
I followed her into the house once again
wondering what the hell I was getting myself into.

Delilah Spelman AKA Miss. Marple

I wonder what those two were fighting about this time? There's no way I bought that drivel the chief had spewed at me, the girl hated my cats, she'd never willingly volunteer to come over to do my hair, the few times she'd done it she had been in an all fired hurry to be gone, that's why I hadn't bothered her again I didn't like making other people uncomfortable.

Well whatever the case may be I got a free hair treatment out of it, and a chance at some gossip, I wanted to know all about that gorgeous hunk of man who looked at our Sam like she was his favorite dessert.

Chapter 16

GABE

I woke with the idea of finally tackling my real purpose for being here, I'd been so caught up in my new feelings for Sam I almost forgot everything else. There were still things that needed doing, like repairs to the house, checking on Charlie's health and making sure these two were set financially. For the next little while at least my flower's welfare was tied up with Charlie's, but if I had my way she would soon be my responsibility.

I found the chief in the kitchen with a bowl of...oatmeal? Gah, I hate that stuff I don't care how good it is for you.
"Morning chief."
"Traitor."
I stopped on my way to the coffee, "Exactly why am I a traitor now?"

"You couldn't have given me one piece of your steak? That thing must've weighed fifteen pounds and you couldn't share just one little piece?"

"I'm pretty sure that's where Sam breaks out her weapon of choice."

"Good to see you're so afraid of one tiny little girl nice to know who'll be wearing the pants in that relationship." Oh he was good, but not good enough.

"Nice try chief but not gonna work, now stop trying to pick a fight with me before I've had my first cup of the day."

"Get me one too will ya." I think he smacked his lips.

"I'm pretty sure caffeine's off your list."

"Come on, you didn't buy that nonsense did you?" I got the puppy dog look.

"Where's Sam by the way?" I actually missed her mouth.

"Genghis Khan is across the street hopefully being mauled by half a dozen cats, serves her right."

"That was mean Charlie, you shouldn't have done

that to her." I was laughing when I said it.
"So, are you gonna give me coffee or not?"
"I don't think so." I leaned back against the
counter as I took my first sip, there next to me
was a covered warming dish with a note with my
name on it.

"Holy..." there had to be a smorgasbord
under there. There was stuffed French toast,
sausage and eggs, home fries, damn. I looked
from my spread over to the chief's bowl of
oatmeal and shook my head.
"How long have you known your daughter now,
and you still pick fights with her when you know
you can't win?"
"Because I'm always hoping to win one, so you
gonna share or not?"
"Share what?"
"Your breakfast what else, I know what's under
there you know, she gave you the good stuff and
stuck me with this disgusting swill. He plopped a
spoon of his cereal back into the bowl.

"How do you know what's under here?"
"Because I watched her make it." He was back to
grumbling under his breath, I picked up the note

pretty sure of what it would say, I was right. "Nothing doing Chief, I have strict orders no coffee and no French toast, just oatmeal and, did you have your juice?" I think he was contemplating killing me.

"Anyway we need to talk." I took my food over to the table and dug in, I think he whined a little. I kinda felt sorry for the guy, but Samantha was pretty explicit in her note about what would befall me if I sided with the enemy. It was nice to know she wanted me in her corner.
"Last time we had one of your talks I ended up in the dog house no thank you." He was sulking now, arms folded and everything .
"Not this time, this time it's about what Phil wanted me to do, what I promised him I'd do." I knew bringing up Phil's name would convince him of how serious I was, I also knew if I told him it's what Phil wanted it might help him accept my help easier. I knew beneath all the comedic banter he was a very proud man and I had no doubt his daughter was the same.

"What is it you have to say son?"
I had no idea, before I came here I had the idea to drop some money maybe exchange numbers and

maybe check in once in a while, now my whole game plan has changed.

First because I really liked these two, they were a vast difference from the people I usually dealt with, in fact outside my family who could sometimes be as quirky as these two, they were the most genuine people I'd ever met. Just like Phil had been, that's why we had been such good friends, having him there was like being home with Jon.

Secondly I think I'm falling in love with my flower, so there was no way my first plan was gonna fly. I'd have to make plans to fly them out often, and since Sam was finished with school that shouldn't be too difficult. I also had to see about the repairs to the house, so far it needed a paint job and the roof might need retiling that I could see.

"Now don't get mad, but I would like to have some repairs done on the house, make sure things are up to code, maybe see about having something installed that would let you go upstairs if you want, and we definitely need to fix up your bathroom down here."

"Ooh, Miss. Priss isn't gonna like that, me coming upstairs, that's been her personal domain for the past few years, I haven't been up there since the accident and Phil well..."

"I know chief." I reached over and patted his shoulder.

"So what do you say, sound like a plan?"

"That's a lot of money son, I don't know."

"Forget about the money, it's what Phil would do if he was here, I'm sure, so I can do no less."

"I guess."

Wow, that was easy I was gonna have to play the Phil card every chance I got.

We heard the rumblings of the tornado right before the slamming of the front door.

"You! Pull that stunt again and I'll chain your chair to the radiator in the bathroom." She was standing in front if him, hands on hips, foot tapping and a storm cloud on her face. Her clothes were also covered in cat hair. The chief had finally got a clue and folded his lips. Wise man.

"Did you give him any of that?"

"Nope." I stuffed my last piece of amazing French toast in my mouth before she had a mind to put me on punishment as well. The chief eyed me and scowled. I guess he'd thought that I was going to share.

"Hey guess what Sam, Gabriel here was just telling me how he should install one of those stair climber things so I could come up there and check on you."

My coffee spewed across the table from my mouth. What the hell, I didn't say that.
"Why would you want to do such a stupid thing?" Now she was mad at me, which I realized from the smug look on his face was exactly what he wanted. Oh really, two could play at this game. "That's not exactly what I said, I suggested it since I thought he would want to see the rest of his home since he hasn't been able to get up there for so long, it was just a thought. I also wanted to fix up his bathroom down here so he would have more room to maneuver, nothing major, just the things I thought Phil would want if he were here." Top that old man.

"Pop that was mean, trying to get the man in trouble when all he's trying to do is help." See, two birds with one stone I averted her anger from me, and got her to accept the repairs in one fell swoop. I just might be able to keep up with my little flower after all.

"Buttercup..." Chief started but she cut him off.

"Shut it, I have to go clean up this mess, look at my clothes." She didn't give him a chance to finish before she left to go upstairs.
"I can't wait to see what you get for dinner." I shook my head at him, he threw a spoon of oatmeal at my head. I kid you not, an almost fifty-year old wheel chair bound man wanted to start a food fight.
I wasn't stupid enough to fall for his ploy though I just cleaned myself and the dishes up and went to wait for her in the living room.

When she came down the stairs I was ready for her, or so I thought, before I saw her freshly scrubbed face and the form fitting tank top and shorts she wore. Fuck me... She's an innocent virgin Gabriel take it easy. That's what I told myself but my body had other ideas. I seriously needed that athletic cup.
I was going to behave myself, I really was, but then she smiled at me. Oh what the hell what's the worst that could happen? I was asking myself this as I got up and walked towards her.
The most that she could do is loosen a tooth or

two, it would be so worth it.

When I reached her, I took her face between my hands, feeling the heat of the blush that was forming there I bent my head slowly giving her time to pull away if she wanted to. Her lips were fucking soft and sweet, like cherries, I tried to eat her lips off her face. That's the only way I could think to put it. The kiss was deep and hard and so fucking good I thought I might cum from just that alone. Fuck if kissing her made me this fucking hot what would being inside her for the first time be like? I couldn't wait to find out. Fuck moving too fast, when you found what you wanted you didn't beat around the fucking bush.

Yeah, but she's young Gabriel, and she's Phil's little sister, tread carefully. That thought helped to pull me back from the precipice but barely. I'll take it as slow as I can, but I wasn't making any promises.

Chapter 17

GABE

My girl likes kissing and she's not shy about it either. All throughout the day she would corner me and devour my mouth. She was such a delightful mix of innocent and siren it left me hot all day.

I couldn't believe how open she was, one minute I would me measuring Charlie's bathroom to get the dynamics and the next my back would my against the wall, and we would be playing tonsil hockey. Her lips were bee stung within two hours, which only made them more kissable. So when she wasn't tackling me, I was tackling her.

The chief's eyes were getting a real work out.

GABRIEL'S PROMISE | 97

Chief

Good Lord the girl is a floozy, every time I turned around her lips were redder and puffier, and the boy had a perpetual stupid ass grin on his face, they think I don't know what they're up to. While I sit here molting away from hunger since Miss. Priss fed me that awful oats and nothing else the two of them are running around here like horny teenagers, you'd think a grown man would have more control.

I was thinking of something to say that would get her hackles up but then I thought better of it, maybe she'd be in a better mood and I could finally get a proper meal around here.

SAM

Wow, I really like this kissing stuff, how come no one ever told me how good that felt? And my Gabriel must be an expert at it cause he always made me feel so good. He must've had a lot of practice I didn't like that thought one bit. No sirree Bob, not, one, bit.

I wonder if he had a girlfriend back home. He better not...we'll just see about that.

Maybe I needed pop's shotgun for this, last I saw it was in the kitchen.

Chief

I wonder what had Miss. Priss in a tizzy
now, I saw her come and lift the shotgun off its
hook, I didn't hear anyone pull up outside so it
could only mean one thing.
I thought of giving Benedict Arnold a heads up
but changed my mind, served him right whatever
it was, knowing Ma Barker it was probably
nothing more than breathing the wrong way.
I rolled my chair closer to the doorway between
the kitchen and living room so I could hear what
was going on.

GABE

I was in the chief's room getting some measurements when I heard the unmistakable sound of a shotgun being cocked behind me, what the hell?
I turned around to such a sight as to make a lesser being piss themselves; what the hell had happened now? Not five minutes ago she had cornered me for another one of her tongue attacks now she was pointing a gun at me.

"You got a girlfriend in Virginia?"
"What?" What the hell was she talking about?
"You heard me Casanova."
"Of course not, if I did I wouldn't be here kissing you what kind of man do you take me for?"

"Yeah right, maybe you think you can have a little tryst with the country hayseed before going back to your city hussy." She actually sited me, no joke, gun on shoulder finger on trigger and eye squinted. Right at my head; again what did I get myself into?

"Samantha I'm not that type of man, now put down that gun before someone gets hurt."
She took her sweet time lowering the gun before she turned and went back the way she came and I breathed a sigh of relief, which lasted all of two seconds. I was going to have to teach flower a thing or two about dating etiquette.

I followed her to the kitchen where the chief was sitting in the doorway grinning like an ass. I took her hand and dragged her out the backdoor into the yard.
" The next time you point that thing at me I'm going to tan your hide."
"Oh yeah, you just try it, I'll punch you in the eye."
She would too the infuriating woman.
"I mean it Samantha, you don't kiss a man half to death one minute and then point a gun at his head the next, not unless you're crazy."
"Don't you call me crazy." Oh shit now she was fuming which was never a good thing.

How to calm her the hell down? The chief was no help he was once again watching and laughing like he was at the damn movies. No wonder my flower petal was half crazy cause her father was all the way nuts. Funny! I never noticed anything off about Phil.

"Okay what set you off this time?"

She started blushing and bowed her head, now she was shy, I found myself looking to the heavens for guidance.

No wonder the chief was always doing it, I'd only known her a few days and already I was looking for divine intervention.

"Well?" I was still holding both her hands in mine so she couldn't get away, or slug me.

"We...ll, we were doing all that kissing stuff and I never stopped to think if you had a girlfriend or not, I don't want to kiss you if you have a girlfriend that's not right."

She was too damn cute and adorable, no wonder I'd fallen so hard so fast. She was my own personal enigma, an innocent lamb in the body of a sexy siren.

"Do you believe me when I say I don't have one?"

"I guess."

"No guessing Samantha, either you believe me or you don't."

She squinted her eyes at me, uh oh I don't think

she liked my tone of voice.
"I'll think about it."
"You'll..."

She was the most exasperating female.
"Okay then, no more kissing until you do figure it
out." She pouted at me and I turned and walked
away; the chief was smirking and I wanted to kick
his chair but that couldn't be right so instead I just
gave him a glare as I passed him by.
"If I had any sense I'd pack my bags and get out of
this asylum." I muttered it as I made my way pass
him, which only made him laugh harder. I went
back to doing what I was doing for another ten
minutes.
When I came out of the room Charlie was in front
the television and Billie the kid was in the kitchen
supposedly making dinner, there was a lot of
banging and grumbling going on in there though.

"Pssst, what'd you do to set her off?"
"As If you weren't listening."
He cackled at that one.
"Lord you two are a pair, I hope I live through this
courtship of yours boy, you know kisses are
supposed to soften the girl up not turn her into a

spitting hellcat, looks like you need some help. I thought you big city types knew all about the birds and the bees."

"Shut it." Lord now I was beginning to sound like her.

We watched the game for a little bit before Sam came into the room.

"Lord here come the kissing bandit." He muttered that out the side of his mouth, right before a whirlwind landed in my lap.

"I believe you." She hurried the words out and then her lips were on mine.

I forgot all about chief being in the room for a second as we just kissed like two horny teenagers.

"If you two don't cut it out, I'm gonna throw cold water on you."

Sam stiffened up I guess she just remembered we had an audience too; good to know I could make her forget herself.

"Pipe down if you want something more than cauliflower for dinner." She huffed back out of the room.

"No indeed son you're not doing it right, there's no softening far as I can see, you have your hands full with that one. Now tell me this since you introduced her to this new pastime of locking lips, who's she supposed to kiss when you head out? Cause my girl is the practice make perfect type."

Chief

That was a plain and utter lie, if anyone of
these yahoos around here tried to kiss the Venus
flytrap she would take their heads off, but he
didn't have to know that. Serves him right for not
sharing his breakfast and I knew just how to stoke
the flames.
"Maybe she'd ask Brand to help out, those two
learn practically everything together." I sat back
and awaited the explosion, it wasn't long in
coming.
"The hell she would, she wouldn't dare." I just
raised my brow at him doing everything I could to
keep a straight face.
He was out of the chair like a shot, uh oh maybe I
shouldn't a said anything who knows how Miss.
Priss would react.
All I heard was a loud screech followed by
po...op. Shit that boy sure had a big mouth.

Chapter 18

GABE

The next couple days were mild by Holder standards; the cold front had warmed somewhat and the grumblings were down to a minimum, if not completely gone.

This is Sam and Chief we're talking about here after all I think grumble is their language of choice. My flower is still practicing her kissing skills on me, and there's been no more mention of the Brandon kid. Good one chief.

I've been ever so gently getting Sam use to the idea of coming home with me for a visit, the chief too of course, it just wouldn't be right without him, besides I don't think they were ready for that type of separation yet.

I took Sam into Annandale for something to do since chief was going fishing with Geoffrey and I told him I had no interest in that, at which time he questioned my manhood.

She needed new books anyway and I wanted to look around, it got me to thinking about where she got her spending money. They must live off of the chief's disability I think. That can't be much, especially with a teenaged girl to support, from what I can tell they love to shop.
That's the first thing I have to take care of, padding their account; I'm sure they'll both raise hell so I'll have to find a diplomatic way to broach the subject. I think I know just how to do it too.

We walked around for a while after she got her books until we came across a pet store and she got all dreamy over this puppy in the window, she'd been wearing a scowl the whole time we were here until now. I'd come to realize that was her people repellant, it worked too.
Seeing her become so soft over the dog there was only one thing I could do.

When we got home hours later laden down with half the pet store Charlie was already back. He came out on the porch as we were leaving the car.

"What the hell is that?" He pointed to the obvious dog in Sam's hands.

"It's a dog, what does it look like?" she went into warrior stance, feet planted, chin lifted, ready for battle.

"Whose dog?"

"Mine, Gabriel got him for me, isn't he cute?"

"Looks like a squirrel with hair to me, where do you think he's supposed to stay?"

"With me and don't you say one word about my Charlie."

"Char...you named your damn dog after me?

"He's a king Charles what else would I name him?"

Oh good Lord I hope she wasn't serious about that.

"I'll cook him if you bring him in this house."

Now that was just mean, nasty and mean.

"I'll feed him to you."
Wow, okay.

"Nobody's cooking the damn dog, could you two act like adults for once?"
They both turned the Holder glare on me. Yikes! I held my hand up in surrender.
"Carry on." Now I was the one rolling my eyes as I followed my flower inside, these two surely were a pair.
As I passed the chief to get to the door he had one last parting shot.
"I hope that mutt eats your expensive shoes, and don't ever forget your car door open, if you know what I mean."
"You're a mean old man, I think I'll leave Charles down here with you tonight."
He spluttered all kinds of threats but I kept going, maybe I could get Sam to feed him cauliflower for dinner again.

Chapter 19

Chief

" That's it, I'm taking this mutt out to the woods and setting him free." Damn dog kept me up all night with his yapping , that damn Gabriel was more trouble than he was worth. Buying her a dog, like I didn't have my hands full with one pain in the ass already.

"Don't you threaten Prince Charles or you'll be the one in the woods."

"Samantha Eliza Holder don't you threaten me , and where in the blazes is that upstart I thought you two were joined at the lips?" I got a dishcloth thrown at my head for my efforts.

"You rang chief?"

I rolled my eyes at him, he was such a traitor; some son in law he was going to be.

"We have to do something bout that damn dog, if he sleeps down here again I won't be held responsible for my actions." Look at him with that

smirk, I'll get him back before the day was out. Now instead of one enemy in the camp I had two, I would've thought the boy would be on my side, but no he had to side with Calamity Jane.
"What seems to be the problem chief?"
"Wha... first of all why was that dog down here? Shouldn't the flying squirrel be up in Miss. Priss's room since she's so in love with him?"
"Pop Prince Charles probably just wandered down the stairs in the middle of the night and couldn't find his way back up, when I fell asleep he was right there with me."

I looked at traitor Joe and caught him smiling, I knew he had made good on his threat and let that damn dog down here.
"What were you doing in Samantha's room last night Gabriel Sweeney?"
Good Lord the boy is always spraying me with coffee.
"What?"
"Nothing, I just thought I heard you moving around in there last night I followed the foot steps over my head from your room to hers. You're lucky my legs don't work or I would've been up those stairs with my shotgun." Good she was

glaring at him with murder in her eyes. *My work here is done.*

GABE

Oh you're slick chief I could see my cactus bristling already, there had to be some way to get out of this.

"Oh you must've heard when I went to the bathroom, the two rooms are so close you must've been mistaken, besides I listened outside the door to see if Charles was crying, you know new surroundings, new faces he might've had a hard time adjusting, but I didn't hear a peep so I went back to bed, I guess he'd already come downstairs to find grandpa."

"Aw, that's so cute, hear that pop you're grandpa."

I looked at him and he was cross eyed with frustration, gotcha.

"What's for breakfast Samantha would you like some help?" She preened under my attention, as the chief went back to rolling his eyes and muttering.

"That's okay, you sit and have your coffee, I've got it all under control." She turned back to the stove with the dog underfoot.

I took the opportunity to give the chief a wink while stifling a grin, he'd gotten steamed veggies again for dinner last night, only this time she'd added boiled fish, I didn't even want to know. Yuck. You would think he would learn his lesson by now, but no, he still kept putting his foot in his mouth.

There was a knock on the door and I sat at attention, I hope it wasn't a salesman it was too early in the morning for this mess.
Whoever it was must not have been a stranger because I heard the door open and two sets of feet came towards us. I saw the chief looking rather jovial all of a sudden and thought it was his fishing buddy, but no, when the new arrivals entered the kitchen I understood his sudden joy. He was mean, dog mean.

"Good morning Holders." They went over to kiss his cheeks one on each side.
"Thanks for calling us in Charlie, we all know how difficult she can be about these things."
Diana and Paula looked at me while waving their hands in Sam's direction.
Uh oh, chief what the hell did you do now? I think

I heard the sound of a locomotive coming from the stove where Sam stood, but no it was just my wildflower growling.

Chief

Well now what was I supposed to do? These
two were ganging up on me left and right so I
called in reinforcements couldn't' have Miss.
Priss and her new sidekick winning all the battles
now could I?
"So Sam have you decided what style you want?
I'm not sure about the blonde thing though, I mean
I just never saw you as a blonde but whatever, if
that's what you want I say go for it."
I forgot how much and how fast that Thorpe girl
could talk.

"What in the Jiminy crickets are you talking
about Diana Thorpe and what pray tell are you
doing in my house before the butt crack of
dawn?"
"Actually sweet daughter mine it's almost eight,
and I know I taught you how to treat guests; grab
a seat girls Gabriel here never got a chance to talk
to you lovely young ladies the other night since
so...me...body was hogging him."

"Oh hi again Gabriel, how do you like our little town?"

SAM

I knew what this was about it's because I've been feeding him veggies and now I'd named my dog after him, those are the only reasons I could think of why he would subject me to these two imbeciles first thing in the morning.
That fool Paula was primping and preening already and who the hell wore stilts to walk around the corner?
"I repeat what are you talking about?" If she didn't stop making eyes at him I was going to pluck them out her head.

I guess my voice must've alerted Prince Charles to my displeasure, because no sooner had I finished speaking than he was attacking their ankles.
I laughed my tail off at their screeching and hopping around, pop covered his face with his hands and Gabriel was trying not to laugh but losing.

"At least it's better than buckshot, now you two get going, I wouldn't let either of you near my head if I was going bald and you had the cure and don't think I don't know why you're really here. Paula go husband hunting somewhere else and as for you hot pants I thought you were so in lo...ve with Dan Young? Why, are, you, here? " They didn't move fast enough to suit me so I did what I did best.

"Samantha Eliza, have you lost your cotton-picking mind? Put that thing down, go ahead on girls she's not right in the head this morning, maybe another time."
"Lord why you don't listen to me when I talk to you, I asked you to make her sweet, now she's worse than ever and to top it off she brought in a ringer." Pop was beseeching the heavens again, he does that a lot.
"As for you, humph, I don't even know where to start." I pointed at him, he looked nervous as well he should, this last stunt was just too much.

Chapter 20

GABE

Well it's been two hours since this morning's theatrics; I give it until about midday before the next fireworks session commences.
The chief has been in hiding the coward, leaving me to deal with Sam's wrath which may I remind you was all his doing.
She's been on the rampage ever since and it seems she handles her anger by cleaning. I tried my best to stay the hell out of her way, while Prince Charles followed her and the vacuum around yipping and jumping like he thought it was a fun new game.

The mutterings were back in full force, I wouldn't want to be in those two girls' shoes when she finally caught up with them I'll tell you that much.
I heard some pretty vicious threats being thrown around; one of them apparently was going to be

shanghaied to the Orient, while the other would be wearing the scarlet letter. I have no idea which century my flower lived in in her head, but she had their punishments all mapped out nice and proper.

At about one, when I was beginning to think peace would rein the chief stuck his head out of his bedroom door yelling something about lunch and starving invalids. Since I was upstairs I only heard the crash and the 'son of a', so I'm guessing she beaned him with something.
I peeked over the rail and even Prince Charles had stopped his running around and was just standing off to the side, probably waiting to see what his crazy mother would do next.
"Samantha?"
"Gabriel."
"Did you kill him?"
"Would you help me bury the body?"

"I heard that, what kind of daughter talks that way about her poor old man? I was just trying to help, you could do with a new hair styling if you ask me. All that wild hair is what makes you so ornery that's what I'm thinking. In the old days where you seem to live by the way Belle Starr, they would've cut it all off to release demons. I'm

thinking it's long past due."
Why didn't the man shut up? I have to get down
there before she really does him in. I grabbed her
as soon as I got down the stairs and laid one on
her. She was full of piss and vinegar and it added
some spice to our tongue action.
I loved the way she just dropped everything when
I kissed her, the way her body molded itself to
mine as if she couldn't get close enough.

"Behave yourself." I whispered as I kissed
her nose. It was hard to believe that the hellcat
could become so pliant from just a few kisses. I
was really looking forward to taking her home
with me for a good long visit. I'd finally gotten
her to agree to come with me as long as the chief
could come along. I think she didn't want to be
apart any more than I did. I had to call mom soon
and maybe warn her of her prospective future
daughter in law and her penchant for the
eccentric.

"If you two are done sucking face, there is a
little matter of lunch to be discussed seeing as
how I never got to finish my breakfast because
Wyatt Earp out there lost her damn mind. I still

have friends down at the station you know, all it would take is one phone call to have you up on charges of abuse and neglect and after all my years of hard work taking care of that harridan." Of course the coward said all of this from behind the safety of his door. Samantha, who I'd just calmed down with kisses was spitting mad again and looking around for something, Lord knows what and I didn't want to find out.

So I started all over again, only this time I upped the ante a little, by ever so gently letting my finger graze her breast. She almost swallowed my tongue as she purred and rubbed herself against me. I guess she liked it. Good times.

Chapter 21

GABE

My mom was chomping at the bit to get her hands on my girl, I'd given her a brief preview of what was coming her way and she'd laughed her ass off.
She'd even talked to the chief for a little bit, at which time he proceeded to lie his ass off, according to him Sam and I were termagants who spent all our time making his life a living hell, how I got included in the equation was anybody's guess.
She promised to make it up to him when I took them home in a few days.
She wanted to have a little party to welcome them but I begged her to hold off on that, I needed to give my girl a few days to settle in before releasing her among Virginia's elite, not because I was embarrassed by her, but because I had no doubt she would have even less tolerance for their bullshit than I did. I figured giving her a few days

to get use to her new surroundings would be the best way to go.

"You plan on turning Miss. Priss loose in polite society? Good luck with that."
"Shut it chief."
"Don't say I didn't warn you, your family own any firearms son?"
"Yes why?" He gave me the 'you're being an ass' look.
"Any blondes liable to be hanging on to you, any Mrs. Sweeney hopefuls back in the big city?"
"Not that I know of."
"You better be sure because if I know my little cherry blossom there'll be hell to pay. From what I can tell the little woman has decided to lay claim to you, what with all the kissing and carrying on going on around here lately." He turned up his face.

"One thing I know for sure, she sure as spit don't share worth shit, almost took poor Phil's eyes out when she was three for taking piece of her Halloween candy. You got your hands full with that one let me tell you, but remember this sale is final, no returns no exchanges. I do feel sorry for your poor mama though, she sounds like a beautiful woman, too bad she's about to meet Cerberus." He shook his head like that shit was funny.

"I'm telling her you called her a three headed dog from hell."

"You would." He rolled his eyes at me.

We heard Sam and Prince Charles returning from their walk, she's been in a much nicer mood the last couple days after I'd convinced her to ease up on her father and I've been bribing her with kisses. He was once again allowed grown up food, but knowing his penchant for getting her riled who knew how long that would last.

"Hey guys, let me go wash up and I'll start lunch." She placed the dog in the chief's lap with a mischievous smile.

He wanted to say something, I could see him biting his lip to keep it all inside, he actually made it until she left the room, I was so proud.

"What the hell is this thing supposed to be anyway? If you were going to get a dog couldn't you get a more masculine dog? All this thing is good for is eating and yipping it's damn fool head off."

"It's Sam's dog , she didn't want a masculine one."
"You're such a wuss."
"Whatever, at least I get to eat like a grown up."
"Sell out, you need to turn in your man card, she's
got you stupid, what's next, you gonna play tea
party with her and the mutt?"
"If that's what she wants."
"What...? You...? What happened to the soldier
that came to my door last week?" He was back to
shaking his head at me as if I were a lost cause.
"If you keep messing with me I'll tell her about
the Cerberus crack, I think she was marinating
prime shell for dinner, you know what that
means." I knew that would shut him up.

Chapter 22

GABE

The only well- behaved one of the bunch was the damn dog. He seemed to take to traveling rather well for it being his first time.
"Samantha would you like some champagne?"
"Good Lord boy are you mad? Hey Miss, what was your name again young lady I'm sorry?" He asked the flight attendant.
"Julie sir." She answered with a smile.
"You people got any sharp implements around here? Anything that could go boom or the like?"

She looked at him at sea; I would've interrupted but I wanted to see where he was going with this.
"I don't think so sir." The poor girl was looking all kinds of confused.
"Okay then, good."
He sat back again, glaring at his daughter who looked like she was imagining strangling him.

She turned to me with a smile.

"Sure Gabriel, sounds lovely."

"Oh Lord now she's queen Samantha, more like Margot Channing. Fasten your seat belts folks, it's gonna be a bumpy ride." And cue the eye roll.

This man is a real ham; I should really let her have at him if only to get some peace and quiet.

I poured each of us a glass, which my girl promptly put up to her nose and caught the giggles.

"They tickle Gabriel." She's so fucking cute is it any wonder she'd stolen my heart that first day?

"Have mercy, must you always embarrass me, you'd think you've never been civilized, you're supposed to drink it not sniff it Marie Antoinette." I barely saved the champagne flute that she was about to launch at his head.

"Chief!" I said warningly, the only reason Sam was being quiet is because she was afraid of flying, that's why I'd offered her the champagne.

"Wh...at?"

Maybe he didn't need champagne he was crotchety enough as it was. While my attention was turned away, my delicate flower proceeded to down the entire glass of champagne in one full swoop.

The giggles really started then, followed by the hiccups, then the burps, which sent the chief into a tizzy.

"I can just see it now, Summer Sweeney, meet Blanche Dubois, I'm never gonna live this down." He shook his head looking all kinds of put upon while I looked above for guidance.

If I survived this plane ride it would be a miracle.

GABE

Chief for all his big talk was asleep in the bedroom within twenty minutes, while Sam attacked me in my seat.
I had to relegate the staff to the outer room because she got a bit...let's just say the kisses were hot and heavy. I'll have to remember what alcohol did to her. No drinking for my baby in public.
"Gabriel?"
"What baby?" I was nuzzling her neck giving us a chance to breathe, she was lethal with that tongue.
"You're too far away."
"What do you mean, I'm right here."
"But I can't feel you."
Aha, she was straddling my legs and her tight jeans and the bucket seats didn't allow her to get the friction she needed.

Other than kissing this was her new favorite thing, rubbing herself against me until I was hard enough to cut diamonds . I didn't complain though, I let her enjoy her new -found pleasure at my expense, though every night it was becoming harder and harder not to rub one out.
She was so innocent she had no idea what she was

doing to me.

I especially liked to see the look of amazement that would sometimes cross her face when she felt something new.

I couldn't wait for the first time I brought her to orgasm while buried inside her.

For now I just tried to help her out with her dilemma.

I reclined the seat all the way back so she was lying on top of me.

"Hmmm." She growled like a wanton and had me ready to shoot off in my pants like a green boy.

Fuck she was climbing my body to get that friction just where she needed it.

I tried to calm her down since her father was in the other room asleep thank heaven, Lord knows what would be coming out of his mouth if he caught us.

Chapter 23

GABE

We're here, finally, the ride home in the limo was a trial in patience ; the chief was in rare form with the innuendos and eye rolls I'm guessing he hadn't been as asleep as I thought. He was being more of a pain in the ass than usual; thank heaven my flower petal was too buzzed to catch on to half of what he was saying. And why was she buzzed? Because after our hot and heavy make out session I had to excuse myself to the bathroom, at which time she finished the last glass of bubbly.

To top it off Prince Charles had finally had it with being cooped up all day and was letting his displeasure be known.

"Come on baby we're here." I tried helping her out of the car, my baby was blitzed.

"We are? Oh Mylanta, Gabriel you live here alone?" She was gaping at my home.

"Yep." And if I have my way you'll be living here too very soon, I kept that little tidbit to myself for now though, one thing at a time.

        "What are you, the country cousin come to town?"
"Chief!"
"Wh...at?"
"Cut it out."
"Yeah pop, cut it out, we're about to meet Gabriel's family, have to be on our best behavior." She put her finger up to her lips in a silencing motion.
"Whatever you say Mata Hari, it's too late for you not to embarrass me, sloshed out of your mind and it's not even noon yet."
"Oh shush you I'm not, what's that word, oh hey where's Prince Charles?"
"He's in your hands Mae West."

        He turned to me after his last insult to her, I guess it was my turn now.
"See what you've done? I told you not to give her any fancy champagne, but do you listen noooo, now we all have to take a ride on the crazy train,

if you think she's a handful when she's sober, wait until you get a load of this mess. You better tell your family not to come here today unless you want to ostracize every last one of them."

"How do you know, you've seen her like this before?" She was singing to the dog now and swaying from side to side.
"Once when she got into the cherry brandy, I think she was fifteen, Lord love a duck, I had to call Geoffrey over to see to her."
" She seems happy enough to me."
He snorted.

"Okay, don't say I didn't warn you."
Just then I saw my dad's car pulling through the gates, I should've known mom won't be able to wait.
Oh well how bad can it be?
"You got a video camera in that mausoleum boy?"
Now he was insulting my house.

"Yeah, why?" what the hell's he up to now.
"Because I want to document this for prosperity, because sure as spit it's gonna be one for the

books."

"I doubt it'll be that bad, especially if you leave
her alone." I gave him a warning look but who am
I fooling? The irascible old goat won't listen to
me.

I turned back to Sam who was now trying to braid
the dog's hair. Alrighty then.

Chapter 24

GABE

My family pulled up and came towards us, I thought I saw a worried frown pass over the chief's face for a brief second before it was gone, I wonder what that was about?
My little sister Jennifer made a bee line for Sam and the dog, I started to intervene but was interrupted by my parents.
I made the introductions to the chief and turned to Sam just in time to see her giving Jennifer a very weird look. Oh Lord, what now?

"Are you on something?" Sam was looking Jenny over like there was something wrong with her, my sister can be a bit exuberant, a little high strung if you will and I'm not sure that that's a good mix right now not with Samantha sloshed as she was.
"Excuse me?"
"I asked if you're on something."

"No why do you say that silly?"
"Because you can't stay still and you're talking a mile a minute." Dad started to laugh I don't know what the hell he found funny about this. I glared at chief when he started humming the theme song from twilight zone. If my mom wouldn't have a fit I would've kicked his chair. So I just leaned over and whispered in his ear.

"I'll lock you in the attic I swear."
" Good luck with that, who's going to help you with the happy drunk then huh?"
"You'll probably be more of a hindrance than a help."
I tuned back in to hear Jennifer laughing off Sam's insult, that's my sister for you, jovial to the bone.
"Come on Samantha we have so much to talk about. "

"Excuse me do I know you?"
"I'm Gabriel's sister Jennifer silly, I just told you."
"If you call me silly again I'll pop you one."
"Okay dirty Harry calm down we have company."

The chief rolled himself over to the girls while I held my face in my hand.

"Son what did you give that poor girl to drink?"
"She was too nervous to fly mom so I gave her some champagne."
"I'm thinking you might not want to be doing that again anytime soon son."
" Thanks for the heads up dad, though you seem to find it funny."
"She's adorable, what do you think Summer, should we go meet our new daughter?"
Well hell.

I followed behind them as they approached the trio who seemed to be having some sort of debate.
"I'm telling you chief Holder, with just the right shade of lipstick she'd be stunning."
"And I'm telling you Jenny, that you can't put lipstick on this particular pig because it will bite your head off."
What the hell were they talking about?
I guess chief forgot he was sitting within reach of Sam when he called her a pig because she set Prince Charles on his head.

"Get that damn rat off my head before I skin him while you're asleep." Of course she didn't take too kindly to that.

"You even think about it and I'll fix your chair so it doesn't lock. "

"Mr. and Mrs. Sweeney I give you my delightful daughter Jane Hudson, aka 'Whatever happened to baby Jane'?"

You've got to be kidding me.

Chapter 25

Chief

I'm worried for my girl , none of these yahoos better not say a bad word to her or I'll be the one looking for the nearest gun cabinet, my baby might have her quirks but she's a good kid. I don't think the boy would let anybody hurt her though, he's worst than a clucking hen with her chicks.

Ever since we got here he's been hovering around her like he was afraid she would disappear, more like he was afraid she would get into the liquor supply.

I hate to admit it but my daughter's a lush, I've never seen such a spectacle in all my days.

Jenny seemed to be a nice enough girl but I was afraid if she didn't dial it down a notch Miss. Priss might deck her one.

The boy's parents were nice enough, father seemed taken with my girl, wait until the first time she lit into him, then we'll see.

"Oh lord what now?" I heard the commotion before I reached the room where Miss. Priss and Jenny were hobnobbing.

"I don't want to go shopping, I hate shopping; shopping is for air headed cumquats who have nothing better to do."

"What's a cumquat?"

"It's a fruit nitwit, maybe if you stopped sniffing paint you might learn something."

"I don't sniff paint Sam, you're so silly."

Oh shit.

"Don't you do it Mary Flora Bell."

"Who's that? I thought Gabriel said your name was Sam?"

"She was a young serial killer in England, well she killed two boys supposedly so I don't know why that makes her a serial killer, again, if you lay off whatever drug of the week you're on you might know these things."

"Uhhh, Sam, I don't think anybody knows these things."

"Well I do."

"And I swear she's not on wacky weed, she just acts like it."

"Shut it."

Where's that son in law of mine anyway, he

knows better than to leave Attila the Hun alone with his little sister, the girl can't weigh but eighty pounds wet, if she pisses off Miss. Priss she's liable to knock her clear into next week.

Chapter 26

GABE

I heard the chief mumbling to himself as soon as I reached downstairs, I'd been up in my study playing catch up on some of my work that I'd neglected while away.

Things looked like I expected them to so I could once again concentrate on the craziness that has become my life.

"What seems to be the problem now chief?"

" Are you insane boy, didn't I tell you yesterday not to leave those two alone together?"

Not this again, he was convinced that Sam was going to do Jenny in, which in an aside is another worry I have, the chief and my little sister has somehow become cohorts, that in my book can't be too good. Jenny is a minx when she wants to be and the last thing my flower needs is for her

pop to bring in reinforcements.
"They'll be fine as long as you don't play the meddling old woman."
He glared at me and rolled his eyes.
"Listen clueless wonder, Jenny is hell bent on taking our girl shopping for this soiree you're planning to have tonight, Miss. Priss is not in the least interested, to hear her tell it, Jenny's leading her off to the guillotine, I should be so lucky."
"You're a mean old man, she doesn't have to go shopping if she doesn't want to mom already has it covered."

I walked into the room just in time to see a hard cover book go flying at my sister's head, and though I've wanted to throttle her a time or two myself in the past I couldn't let my prickly pear bean her.
"Samantha what are you doing?"
The chief of course is now sitting in the doorway shaking his head at me as if the whole thing is my fault.
"Tell her to leave me alone before I drop her out a window, what is it with her anyway? I don't want to go to no stinking salon."
"Gabriel I just thought it would be nice for her to be pampered a little before the party, you know

nails, hair, the works."

"You want to cut my hair..."

"Nobody's cutting her damn hair, and she doesn't have to go anywhere, mom's bringing someone over which you would know Jenny if you'd gone home.

My sister has been camped out in my house for the last two days, which would not have been a problem in itself, except she seemed to spend a lot of time plotting with the chief and flower spent all her time hiding from her.

With all the traffic around here I'd hardly had a chance to kiss her the way I like. Time to put a stop to that mess.

"Boy we don't have time for that now we have things to discuss."

Damn, chief must've caught me leering again. I gave a deep sigh, told Sam to behave herself and gave her a smooch before following him out of the room, Lord knows what was on his mind now, he's been acting a little strange since we got here, even for chief.

I led him to my downstairs library and closed the door, he got right to it.

"Who all is coming to this party son?"

"Friends of the family, why?"

"I don't know about Miss. Priss around all these strange people nothing good can come of it, you have seen her in action right?"

"What are you so worried about? You act as if she doesn't know how to act in public, I happen to think my girl has excellent manners."

"Are we talking about the same person or are you sniffing Jenny's paint? If we're talking about my kid, there's no way this shindig is going off without a hitch, and please in the name of all that's holy don't give her any of that champagne again."

He had a point about the champagne, but as for the rest he was wrong, I know my flower can be a bit...acerbic, but from our talks I also knew she has the etiquette of a seventeenth century schoolmarm.

"I think she'll be fine as long as no one bothers her." I gave him a pointed look.

"Now what's really bothering you?" He fidgeted in his chair for a bit with a look on his face that I hadn't seen before.

"What if your hoity toity friends don't like her?" The words were barely above a whisper.

And there you have it, I don't think I've ever seen the chief look so soft, he was really worried about his daughter.

"They'll love her, what's not to like, she's beautiful, smart and sweet."

Now he's looking at me like I'm the crazy one.

"Have you met my daughter, you know Shotgun Sue, the one who likes to pepper people with buckshot?"

"Well, there's none of that around here so we should be fine, now if you're done worrying like an old woman I have to go get her ready for mom and the stylist."

"This ought to be good, let the games begin."

I took Sam from the parlor room where she was once again questioning my sister's drug intake and led her to my office, this was a delicate situation and needed to be handled with care, I remember only too well the debacle that transpired the last time someone tried to groom her.

I'd barely closed the door before she had me trapped against it in a lip lock.

"Baby!"

"Hmm."

"I have to talk to you about something." I was still returning her kisses though damn I'd missed her mouth.

"Sammy, wait a minute baby." I tried to stem the flow before things got out if hand and I forgot what I'd brought her in here to say.

"Uh huh." she was still trying to recapture my mouth, oh what the hell I'd missed this. I kissed her until her lips were puffy and her eyes were glazed, good, she should be in a more amenable mood now. This might work.

"Mom's on her way over here with a stylist, they're going to bring you some dresses and you can choose whatever you want okay? They're also going to be doing your hair and nails."

"Doing what to my hair and nails?"
Uh oh she looked ready for battle again, more
kisses coming up, it was a crap thing to do but a
man's gotta do what a man's gotta do.
When she'd finally gone all soft and pliant I got
her to agree to the afternoon's beauty fest, her
only stipulation and I quote 'as long as the dress
doesn't make me look like a trollop I'll wear it."
Can't ask for more than that.

Chief

Well it's been an hour since Summer and that Petra woman went off somewhere with Miss. Priss, I haven't heard any screaming, no gunshots fired, I guess everything was okay, but with my harridan that could change any minute.
I hovered around downstairs too nervous to do anything else, that fool boy had gone and got me a monkey suit, what was wrong with my flannels and jeans was beyond me, but apparently these people didn't have much sense, they rather button themselves up to kingdom come and be uncomfortable. I'm only doing it because he said it was for my Sam.

"Chief come on it's time for your trim."
That Jenny is a doll, why my menace couldn't be more like her was beyond me.
"Okay Jenny." I gave one last look to the stairs and followed her to my room, boy had way too much house for one person if you ask me.
She soaped up my face for my shave, such a sweet girl, and set out what she was going to need to fix

me up as she called it.

"Jenny what are these people like that would be here tonight?"
"They're fine I guess, it's not going to be too many, only twenty or so, mom said she didn't want to overwhelm you and Sam."
"Only...Lord love a duck, get your brother in here."
"I can't I have to get thus stuff off your face, besides I think he left for a while."
Lord help us all Miss. Priss would kill one of these high society yahoos if they looked at her wrong, what was that boy thinking? Twenty or so people? I thought it would be five at the most. Oh well nothing I could do about it now.

Chapter 27

GABE

Well it's show time, the guests will be arriving in half an hour, the caterers were set up and ready to go, music was piping through the surround sound speakers and everything was going as planned. All we needed now was for the girls to come downstairs.
My brother Jonathan and his wife Darlene had just arrived, they'll only be in town for the night since Jon had an away game in a couple days.

"Hey lil bro where's my new sister? I hear she's a firecracker, dad seems impressed."
"Hey Jon." I gave him a hug before kissing Darlene's cheek. They were like the perfect football couple, him big and beefy while she was blonde and svelte.
"The ladies haven't come down yet, this is Charlie, Sam's dad."
"Hey man, how's it going?"

That's Jon he never met a stranger. They were
soon arguing football while Darlene tried
pumping me for information.
I heard movement on the stairs and turned in time
to see a vision descending.

"Holy..." I caught myself before I said
anything else out loud.
She looked fucking amazing, they'd done
something to her hair, straightened it I guess, it
was just this waterfall of sleek shiny mass
tumbling down her back behind her shoulders.
The dress was a white one shoulder that hugged
her body to below the hips, then flowed to her
ankles. The redness of her hair was more
pronounced against the whiteness of her dress and
just made her stand out even more: as if she
wasn't gorgeous enough already.

She was wearing heels, not too high but
heels nonetheless I had to remember to ask mom
how she pulled that one off.
I met her at the bottom of the stairs too
dumbstruck to speak at first, I was almost tongue
tied.
"You look extremely beautiful baby." I whispered

it in her ear.
I'd half expected her to be nervous but I didn't
sense anything when I took her hand. The chief
was looking all kinds of proud and I hoped he
kept on his best behavior and kept his trap shut.
Before I could stop him Jon had her up in his arms
swinging her around. Oh Lord, I hadn't had time
to warn him.

"Hey lil sis, you look smashing."
"Jonathan put her down." I rescued her, or him I
wasn't sure which.
"Is that pigskin?"
She'd taken to calling him that after I told her
what he did for a living, Darlene of course started
laughing her ass off, since she too tended to agree
with Sam, she said she had no interest in the game
and she'd married him for his looks not what he
could do on a football field.

"Hello Sam, I'm Darlene, pigskin's wife."
Flower blushed beet red but shook her hand.
In all the commotion I had missed mom and
Jenny's entrance, Jon was looking put out that
Sam wasn't impressed with him but the chief was

making up for that.

The whole family had gathered by the time guests started to arrive, mom had worked on the guest list so I had no clue really who would be here but I had no worries, mom knew what she was doing.

The party was going great, people were talking, dad, Jon and the chief were arguing football, Sam was off in the corner with Jenny and Darlene while mom flitted around making sure everything was just right.

I'd given flower a glass of sparkling cider and told the servers to keep her supplied, so far so good, the chief had been worried for nothing.

About an hour into the party I noticed my girl was giggling a lot more than usual but thought nothing of it, I figured the girls were regaling her with some of my less stellar exploits, or maybe they were laughing at Jon, I'd hardly had anytime with her as people kept pulling us in six different directions but at least she seemed to be having fun. In other words I'd been milling around catching up with old friends when I really just wanted to be with my girl, I thought maybe I could sneak her outside to the garden and steal a few kisses.

The first warning bell came from prince Charles's barking growl. Yes I'd allowed her to bring her puppy, what could it hurt? Besides she said if I didn't let her she wouldn't come downstairs. I figured she could control her dog.

I looked over to see what was going on and was in time to see Sam deck Brenda Winston and knock her on her ass. Oh shit.

SAM

I really like this dress and my hair and my nails, it made me feel like a girl not a simpering ninny mind you, but a girl Gabriel would like. Everyone was being so nice even Jenny wasn't getting on my nerves and Darlene was sweet. I didn't like this new champagne though, it tasted strange and it looked different, I think I had this before but it wasn't champagne.

The next time the guy came around with the tray I took another one. Yep that's the one, it gave me the giggles.
Darlene and Jenny went off to the powder room, why the heck I would need to powder my nose was beyond me.
This lady came up to me all smiles, Prince Charles didn't like her at all, he started puffing himself up in my arms like he was going on the attack.
"So you're the little hayseed Gabriel brought back with him."

"Excuse you!"
"You heard me, whatever made him think you'd

be acceptable here is a wonder, beneath the new spit and polish that Summer no doubt orchestrated you're still a little nobody and don't you forget it."
I laughed it off at first, I mean she was just plain stupid, plus the champagne made me feel good I wasn't going to let her bother me one bit, if she got on my nerves too much I'll let my dog have her, but then she said the wrong thing.
"You do know that Gabriel and I are an item don't you? You do know what that means, it means we fuc..."
That's when I decked the hussy.

Chief

I knew it, I knew it, didn't I tell the boy? Now look, Miss. Priss had gone and killed that woman. People were rushing over to see what the hell was going on and what was Cassius Clay doing, drinking her champagne and smiling like she hadn't a care in the world.

Oh well, the boy had enough money for bail.

Chapter 28

GABE

Mom got to her first but I was hot on her heels. The whole room had gone quiet, while a million things ran through my mind.
First was my baby okay? I mean she was smiling and talking to her dog, but I know my girl.
Second, what the fuck had Brenda said to her? I know Brenda can be a real bitch, her family and mine had been friends for generations, she's been trying to get in my bed since we were sixteen, never gonna happen.

"Sam, baby?" I took her from mom's arms. Darlene and Jenny had made it back from their bathroom run, there were murmurings and whispers all around the room.
I saw some of the snobbish bastards looking at her like she was somehow beneath them and that pissed me off.
"Hey Gabriel." Shit, she was sloshed, if this shit wasn't such a catastrophe I would be laughing my

ass off.

"Baby why did you knock Brenda on her ass?"
She squinted at me as though she didn't
understand my words.

"Who's Brenda?"

I pointed to Brenda who was now being
helped up off the floor, by now dad, Jon and the
chief had joined me and the girls, we were all
surrounding her like a shield, whether
unintentional or by design I wasn't sure, but I
appreciated the show of solidarity from my
family.

"Oh the hussy; she said something bad about my
Gabriel." Now she was playing with my hair, in
the back of my mind I was thinking if I didn't get
her out of this room real fast these people were in
for even more of a show.

Then Brenda started screeching about nine-
one-one and being assaulted, I was about to blast
her but Darlene beat me to it. She started clapping
her hands. I started shaking my head, this wasn't
going to be good.

The chief looked like he was ready to defend her
against all comers and mom was pissed.

"Thank you Sam, I've wanted to knock this tart on her ass for a long time now, try it Brenda, call the cops go ahead, I dare you."
She looked from Brenda to Sam who was now busy nibbling on my neck while I was busy trying to stave her off and not having very much luck.

"What did she say to you slugger?"
"This has nothing to do with you Darlene Dewitt."
"That's Sweeney, which you'll never be, go ahead Sam, tell us."
"She said her and my Gabriel fornicated under consent of the king."
Everyone had a confused look on their face except the chief.

"Lord love a duck, girl would you move into the twenty first century? I blame that homeschooling, that's what it is. I should've made you go sit in a classroom with other kids, at this rate you'll catch up with the rest of the world in fifty years."
"Shut it."
Thank God she was too drunk to come up with anything else, by now my guest were all but baffled.
"Don't tell me to shut it, now tell these people

what this lady said to you, in human terms."

"I can't." she whispered it at him.

He rolled his eyes and looked at me, by now I had figured out the acronym and was ready to deck the lying skank myself.

"That's a lie Brenda and you know it, now tell her the truth." I didn't want to do this here in front of all these people, people that we both knew, that our families knew, but if she forced my hand I would, I wouldn't have my flower thinking for one minute that I would have her in the same room as one of my past flings.

"Oh shit." Dad had just figured it out and whispered it in mom's ear who went even redder with anger.

"Why should I tell this hayseed anything? Who the hell is she but a nobody that you're trying to pass off in our circle...?"

"If that circle includes you it can't be all that great, it would reject a hayseed and accept an adulterous whore? Yes Brenda I know all about you, so go ahead and call the cops, or do anything to interfere with Gabriel and Sam and I will have your business all over this town by noon tomorrow, try...me, let's see who's top bitch."

"It's okay Darlene, she's not going to do anything to Sam, are you Brenda?"
I gave her my stern 'don't fuck with me look." She huffed and walked away, head held high, stubborn to the end. I didn't much care, she would never try anything I'd make her whole family pay and they would never allow that.
Most of the guests stayed but a few left early, good riddance I made note of who they were for future reference. The family was left alone as the remaining guests went back to whatever it was they were doing before the entertainment started.

"Well Lucky Marciano, what do you have to say for yourself? I always knew you were headed for the clinker, but did you have to bring me all the way to Virginia to do it? Couldn't you get arrested back home? Boy you better go get bail money together, and be sure and let them know she's your responsibility while you're at it, speaking of which when do you plan on getting this courtship underway? I would like to enjoy my golden years and at the rate you're going I won't have a moment's peace 'til I'm dead and gone."

" You done?"

"Yep."

"Shut it! Mom I'm sorry to leave you with this but I have to take her upstairs."

"Yes please take her upstairs before you two start carrying on again, it's embarrassing." Chief just couldn't leave well enough alone.

I glared at him to shut him up. Hah.

"See you in the morning Lavinia Fisher."

"Pop you do know I Know who that is right? I think." She put her hand to her head then, I didn't have a clue who that was, then again I never knew what these two were talking about half the time.

I took my flower up the stairs hoping that she'd behave herself at least until we made it to her room.

We got to her room and I faced a new dilemma! Was I supposed to undress her?

Chapter 29

Chief

Well! These Sweeney's have proven their worth, yes indeedy, first the way they gathered around my girl against their mealy mouth friends, and then after Jessica Rabbit had been hauled off upstairs they'd lit into some of them, apparently I'd missed some of the looks some of these yahoos were giving my girl, but Summer sure hadn't. Anyway, I guess what they say is true, money talks, because they were apologizing all over their faces after that, lucky for them raging bull hadn't caught any of those looks or Lord knows how much more damage she would've done. Thank heavens that was over and they were gone.

Well! Looks like I might be making that trip back home alone, yes sir, the boy was a goner if I ever saw one, and my girl, well, I know my little girl, ten sheets to the wind or not, she wouldn't be caught dead manhandling any man like that unless he was the one.
I have to have a talk with her about her behavior

though, the girl didn't seem to have any control whatsoever, it's like when the two of them had me shut up in that bedroom on the plane, I was afraid to come out for fear of losing my eyesight, those two were worst than horny toads, you'd think the boy with all his billions and higher learning would set a better example.

Meanwhile, how did I get stuck with the flying squirrel, if I could get up those stairs I would sneak him into the room, then again, now might be my best opportunity to skin him.
"Don't even think about it chief, give me the damn dog."
Gabriel was muttering ...something under his breath his shirt was partially unbuttoned the jacket was long gone.
I gave him with the gimlet eye.

"Where's hot pants Nellie?"
"Don't start, she sent me after the damn dog."
"Kisses still not doing too good huh? Sum...mer."
I smirked at him because I just thwarted his attempt to kick my chair, he was picking up all of Miss. Priss's dirty habits, I hope she gives him

twice as much hell as she's given me her whole life, though I was gonna miss that little girl.

GABE

If I had any sense I would run as far away from those two as possible, one drove me crazy and the other was just plain crazy.
After I'd asked flower how to get her out of that contraption since I didn't see a zipper or buttons, she'd raised her hands above her head swaying from side to side, humming under her breath.
Yep, plastered, I wonder who the hell gave her champagne? I'd warned the servers not to, oh well, too late to worry about that now.

I'd finally worked the dress up and over her head only to swallow my tongue.
"Sweet merciful heaven." I have to learn to curb my penchant for speaking my thoughts out loud, but damn.
She was wearing a one -piece see through white lace body hugger a la circa nineteen fifties pin up doll, or something. Was my mother trying to put me in an early grave?

Of course by then she was trying to kiss me and climb me, which seems to be her favorite past time when intoxicated. How to be a gentleman in this situation: because this is definitely different from the plane.

There's a bed for instance, a locked door, or at least one that can be locked, and the fact that I don't think I have much control left.

I finally gave in and took her mouth, she was ravenous, and she felt amazing under my hands.

I had to keep reminding myself that there was no way I was going to take advantage of her in this state.

"Gabriel?"
"Yes love."
Without answering she took one of my hand and placed it over her breast.
"It hurts." Geez, I think maybe the chief was right, her education was sorely lacking she had no clue...it would be fun teaching her though.

I rubbed her nipple between my thumb and forefinger and she moaned so loud I swore they could hear us downstairs of course she's now riding my leg trying to get friction.

Her hands moved to the buttons of my shirt and I

tried to help her one handed, there's no way I was giving up the nipple.

When my jacket was gone, again through much machinations, I allowed myself to taste her for the first time, even though it was through lace, I bit down ever so gently and her knees buckled. I loved her innocence, her natural reactions, I wanted them all for myself every last one of them belonged to me.

We'd made it to the bed where I laid fully against her as she made these hot as fuck sounds that had me ready to blow, all while rubbing herself against me and doing her best to inhale my tongue. Go ahead honey it doesn't serve any other purpose.

Her body was amazing, small, compact, firm, I was going to enjoy her for the next fifty, sixty years.

That's right, I had made up my mind, she was mine, and she was gonna stay mine.

"Baby, we have to stop."

She was trying to undo my pants.

"Uh uh."

"Yes babe you're...you've had too much

champagne it wouldn't be right." But boy do I want to.

"No I didn't, I know what you think, it's not true." Of course her words are just a tad slurred.

"What do I think?" I couldn't get enough of that mouth of hers, like strawberries and champagne, hmm.

"You think I'm inebriated."

Well now, if she can come up with that word maybe she's not too far gone after all. Uh huh, cool it Sweeney.

"You're not?" This talking and kissing was kinda fun, it gave us room to breathe.

"No, I'm Sam and you're my Gabriel and my Phil sent you to me."

Well shit, I had to hug her closer after that, my sweet girl, no wonder I'd fallen so hard and so fast, under all the fire and sass, this is who I'd found, my own sweet little flower petal. Of course with my flower nothing ever goes quite the way you expect because no sooner had she made that astonishingly profound statement than she jackknifed in the bed, throwing me off.

"Where's my dog?"

Never a dull moment.

Chapter 30

GABE

I woke up with flower, or should I say under flower, sometime during the night she had crawled onto my body like a limpet and stayed there. I can't even begin to put into words how amazing it feels to awaken like this, I kissed her brow before easing her off of me so I could return to my own room and get ready for the day. Lord knows what kind of mood she's going to be in after last night's theatrics. I got a few mumbles before she settled back into sleep like a little kitten whose claws were sheathed it made me smile. Yep, I'm definitely keeping her, and her loony toons father as well.

I'd made up my mind about that, there's no way I could see separating those two, it seemed almost cruel somehow, I'd just have to buy a mouth cage for the chief to keep his lips clamped shut so he couldn't start any trouble. We'd have to go back to Lexington though to get their affairs in order, pack up the house and do whatever they wanted with it, I doubt chief would want to sell so we'll have to figure something out. Either way they were coming here to stay, if I had to lie my ass off to convince them it's what Phil would've wanted, I'm not above that either.

"Where's the town drunk still sleeping it off?"

I must be crazy to think I wanted to subject myself to this for the rest of my life.

"Can you be nicer when you speak of my future wife?"

"Future...since when? Nobody said anything to me, exactly what went on up those stairs last night boy?"

I ignored him and kept heading towards the kitchen, looks like the whole family was gone for which I was grateful, I needed some down time. I set about making coffee while Rumpelstiltskin did his impression of crazy behind me.

"Would you stop your grumbling? Nothing happened, I just decided that Sam is going to be my wife, and you're both coming here to live with me."

"Boy your light bulb went out? Who says I wanna live with you two? Good merciful heavens, Miss. Priss plus you and the damn dog, what I'm paying penance for pass sins or something? Oh no, you're on your own there son, I'm going back home where I can finally have some peace and quiet, I haven't had any since that girl came home at one week old, she's been hell on wheels ever since then."

"You're coming and that's final."
"Why do I have to come?"
"Because flower would want you to."
"Because flower would want you to." He mocked me.
" What am I her pet monkey? I get to say where I spend my golden years and it ain't in this mausoleum with Heathcliff and Kate."

"Read the classics do you? It doesn't matter what you say, you're staying."
"Way to manhandle the invalid." Now he's sulking.
"Invalid my ass just shut it. You on any kind of punishment?"
He looked at me bewildered.
"Not that I know of why, what did she say I did now?"
His feathers were getting ruffled.

"Nothing, I was just wondering if there was any reason why you shouldn't have French toast."
"You want me to come here and live with not one but now two bullies? No sir uh-uh: show me to the nearest exit, it's time for me to go. Tell her I said it was nice knowing her, I'll be sure and put her crap in the mail and send it to her."
"How you gonna do that? you can't get up the stairs to her room."
"Shit, I forgot about that, oh well, you have enough money around here, take the girl out and buy her some new denims that ought to do it."
"Chief, put a sock in it will ya, now tell me how to go about this marriage thing."

He took so long to answer I finally turned from the stove to look at him. He was staring up at the ceiling, probably asking for guidance again. "What?"
"Boy, you don't have the sense God gave a duck, now here's what you do, you go down to your video store and ask them if they have anything showing how to tame a wild filly, or anything from the animal kingdom, barring that head to the nearest reservation and ask the local Shaman how to go about it, cause you're gonna need all the help you can get."

I was tempted to throw the bowl of egg mix at his head, I really was.

"What the hell are you talking about?"
"Well, marriage is like a type of taming right? So you need to know how to tame that one, as for the actual wedding I would just have her show up on the day and get it over with, cause sure as spit she's going to put up a fuss. I forgot to tell you, she don't cotton too much to marriage, thinks it's men's way of enslaving women. I blame all those classics she reads, Lord knows what those quacks had to say."

I looked at him like he had two heads, was he for real? He couldn't be; and why was I asking him for help? I must really be desperate.
"I know, I'll just withhold kisses until she agrees."
"From what I see around here you could both do with a cooling off, I never thought I'd live to see the day my daughter became a floozy."

I didn't warn him and he got a good slap behind the head for that one.
"Ouch, darn it girl, what you do that for?"
"Watch who you call a floozy." She shook her fist

at him, before turning to me with the most endearing, blushing smile. She wrung her hands in front of her as she came over to me.
"Hi."

"Hi beautiful." I couldn't help myself, I kissed her; of course the peanut gallery had to be heard from.
"Can I have my breakfast before you two start sucking face and forget me again? Now Miss. Priss come here let me talk to you, and where's the flying squirrel?"
She gave him a glare for insulting her dog and went to sit next to him. Yep, I had finally lost my mind if I intended to subject myself to this bedlam.
"He's asleep, how did you sleep pop, everything okay?"
"Stop fussing, everything's fine, now look here, you like Gabriel?"

I guess he was supposed to be whispering, but I heard him loud and clear. She looked in my direction to see if I was paying attention which I of course pretended not to be.
"Yes, why?" She sounded like she was about to

go upside his head.
"Well, you know you're not getting any younger,
soon from now you'll be on the shelf."

Good God the girl was only eighteen, what
was he saying to her? Now I wonder which one of
them is stuck in the seventeenth century.
"Pop, what the blazes are you on about? Are you
sick? Tell me." She grabbed his hands and was
halfway out of the chair before he calmed her
down.

"I'm fine, just fine, but you know, I've been
thinking, and the rain in Lexington have been
bothering me lately, making me more achy than
usual, I talked to Gabriel about it, and he agreed
that we can stay here no questions asked, it's what
Phil would've wanted; but see, the thing is,
Gabriel is an upstanding member of the
community, so he can't have a young unmarried
woman living under his roof, soooooo, we were
thinking maybe you two ought to tie the knot."
She was looking all kinds of confused, and I felt
like I was caught in a scene from Pride and
Prejudice. I did ask for his help though.

"You sold me again didn't you?"
"What, no, what are you babbling about, when
have I ever sold you, I might've thought of it a
time or two, but who would have ya?"
He really was stupid, why the hell he liked to egg
her on was beyond me. She didn't say a word, just
went upstairs and came back with her puppy.
Since there were no fireworks I figured he got off
easy, and at least he got the idea of marriage out
there, convoluted as it was.
It wasn't until I put the breakfast on the table that I
figured out what she was up to. As soon as I put
chief's plate in front of him, she snatched it for the
dog; you can imagine the screaming and hollering
that ensued. Never a dull moment.

Chapter 31

GABE

I spent a week taking these two around, to
my family's horse farm, which Samantha loved,
and we made a nice trip to Colonial Williamsburg,
which I had to practically drag her away from,
among some other landmarks. Later I'll take them
to D.C. to take in the sights but that could wait.
Today it's Virginia Beach, this trip alone has
convinced me that I've lost my marbles, these two
are never going to be anything but what they are,
grumpy, and the chief is the main culprit.

"Pop leave Charlie alone he doesn't want to
look out the window, do you boy?"
"I'm not trying to get him to look out the window
I want to see if the flying squirrel really can fly."
"Chief...! Easy there tiger." I had to grab her
before she choked him of course this is going on
in the helicopter ride over the ocean. Sam insisted

that she wanted to go although I knew she was afraid.

I was sitting next to her holding her hand and kissing her whenever the need arose, while the chief sat across from us with a running commentary.

"Gabriel you know what, remember that nice lady we met yesterday? The one that's a friend of your mom's from that charity thing."

"You mean Bonnie."

"Yes, that's the one, I was thinking we ought to invite her over for dinner sometime soon."

I wondered what the heck that was about, I don't recall Sam being overly enthusiastic when we ran into the woman the day before, and why was chief making slashing motions across his neck?

"If you want to sweetheart, that's what we'll do." Who knows, maybe she wanted to discuss charity works, I'm sure mom would have her involved in that stuff after we were married anyway.

"I'll drop the dog in the water you mark my words."

What had I missed now?

"Chief that's just mean even for you, now what has you in a tizzy this time?"

Neither of them were paying me any mind, they were too busy having a stare down.

"You are a mean spirited little girl, I don't know what I ever did to deserve a daughter who would threaten her poor father."

"Leave my baby alone." She squared off against him.

"Come to think of it, that mutt does look like something you two would produce."

He thought that shit was funny since he was laughing his head off. Sam was whispering to prince Charles, which couldn't be good, right before she set him down.

The damn dog walked over to the chief and peed on his shoe, I looked to the heavens and uttered a prayer while the chief had a conniption fit.

"That's it, first chance I get I'm putting that rat on eBay."

Oh Lord when will he learn? Of course now my house was going to be like a battle station, these two could draw out a war longer than Wellington.

"If you two don't behave I'm going to fix both your wagons." Great Gabriel throw your hat in the ring, you know how flower just hates to be disciplined, hah, I knew just how to get her, him maybe not so much, then again.

"You, if you don't stop with the threats I will invite Bonnie over for every meal of the damn day." He huffed but had the good sense to keep his damn mouth shut. See I'd finally caught on to what she'd been getting at.
I turned to my tiger lily with a sinister smile, she would be the tough one, "No kisses until after we're married."
She folded her arms and rolled her eyes at me, while chief snickered away, which of course earned him a kick to the ankle. So now he had a wet sore ankle, served him right.

"She kicked me, I say she shouldn't get any more kisses for the day."
"You don't get to decide that, that's my job."
"Speaking of which, you figured out how to get Cruella down the aisle?"
Why me?
"Parsnips."

What the hell, what was she talking about now? Apparently the chief knew because his feathers were ruffled and he was chomping at the bit to say something, I guess she won this round because she was smiling.

It's later that night and the house is finally asleep after a long day spent playing referee, now I'm trying to get away from my girls' more amorous attentions, who would've thought that would be the case?
I wanted to wait until after we were married, which she had yet to agree to, but she didn't see anything wrong with trying to attack me.

I know she was still a little innocent so I tried to go slow but she wasn't having it and tonight she seemed even more determined than ever to get what she wanted.
"Baby, we can't." I tried for the one hundredth time to pry her hands away from my zipper.
"Yes we can I'm old enough."
"No Samantha, not until you agree to marry me."

She flopped back on the bed in a huff, I could see her mind working overtime, Lord knows what she would come up with this time, she's had some doozies let me tell you, my favorite was the one about pigs in a blanket.

"Okay, I'll marry you if you do it."
"You're bribing me with sex?"

She was on me again in a flash, hands once again attacking my fly, she was a crazy mix if I ever saw one, on the one hand, conventional, almost puritanical, her ideals were somewhere between Jane Eyre and Anne of Green Gables, but a few kisses and she turned into a Lolita.
I decide to let her have her way, what the hell I wanted it too, so why wait? I'd been willing to wait for her sake but if this is what she wanted, why not? It wasn't too hard to get me on board and after weeks of her innocent torture I was more than ready, hopefully I wouldn't embarrass myself with a weak performance. She's had me so hot for her since the first time she'd flown down those stairs that I was hard pressed to take it easy.

I started off slow and gentle, knowing this was all new for her, her body was amazing, nice and firm and soft, she had soft trimmed curls at her core, soft as silk, she sighed when I touched her there, her hands finding purchase on my shoulders before they roamed over my chest.

I kissed her body, shushing her when shyness threatened to overcome her; I introduced her to the delights of the flesh, as she opened like a flower in bloom.

Our kisses were different somehow, softer, deeper, I let my fingers roam lightly over her shoulders to her neck and down again. Turning her fully onto her back I eased the little silk and lace number she was wearing up and over her head while planting kisses all over her chest. She writhed beneath me, her untried body seeking fulfillment.

"Not yet love." I licked and nibbled my way to her nipple which had become hard and stood upright just waiting for my mouth. Her taste was like nothing I'd experienced before. Her hands came down to grab my hair as I made my way slowly down her body. I licked the crease between her thigh, rubbing the side of my face in the soft growth of hair that was even more red than the one on top.

She made a slight sound when I opened her up with my fingers but I calmed her; she was beautiful her pink flesh glistening with her arousal. Taking care I used jus the tip of my finger to tease her clit.

"Ahhh..." she writhed even harder and pushed herself into my hand. I accepted the invitation and even as I sniffed her taking in her sweet scent I teased her until her l clit peeked out of its little hood. I played around it teasing her before pushing just the tip of one finger inside. "Gabriel."
"I know sweetheart, soon."
"I wanna touch you too."

"I don't think that's good idea baby, I'm hanging on by a thread as it is, if you touch me now it'll be over before we start and you won't get the good feeling, you wan to have the good feeling don't you?"

"Yesss..." She hissed as I licked her with my tongue, I thought for sure she was going to pull my hair out at the roots but I didn't care. I just wanted to have her taste in my mouth. Taking her tight ass in my hands I lifted her to my mouth and sucked on her until she flowed into my mouth. When I was sure that she was ready to take me I climbed up her body and holding her eyes, her head held in my hands I entered her, slowly, gently, ever careful of her innocence. When I felt the little barrier that had kept her intact for me I took her lips in a searing kiss as I pushed through. I accepted her sharp cry into my lungs as I bade me body hold still for her sake so that she could become accustomed to having me inside her.

"I feel so full Gabriel." She moved under me.
"Flower wait...not..." I was talking to myself as she found a rhythm that she liked and moved under me in the most sensuous way I'd ever seen. All that passion and fire was here, her little hands came up and around to pull me down to her mouth once more.

"Kiss me Gabriel." Her voice had gone whisper soft and raspy as she ordered me around, she wasn't shy about telling me what she liked though, and she gave excellent direction. She was everything I thought she would be and more, I can't believe I get to spend the rest of my life with her. Thank you Phil old buddy, I promise to cherish her for always.

She went to sleep in my arms with a smile on her face and I stayed up long after just basking in her glow, not able to keep my hands from her body, her beautiful angelic face, her breast. I played with her to my heart's content as she sighed and moaned in her sleep.

Tomorrow I would have to take care of her she was sure to be sore from her new experience.

I hope to God the chief doesn't figure out what went on up here last night. Oh hell.

Chapter 32

Gabe

She awakened with a smile on her face which I couldn't help but kiss, Uhmm, warm soft Sam.
"Come on love, I ran you a bath." Uh oh, she was feeling frisky again this morning. I couldn't, shouldn't, I'd already turned to her once more in the night, if I took her again she will be sore for sure.
"Stop it baby, you have to take your bath now, or you're going to hurt."
"No I won't."

How did she learn to do that so quickly? That sultry sex kitten voice of hers was going to make a slave out of me yet. I tried prying her arms from around my neck and getting her out of bed but she proved once more just how tenacious she could be. Shit okay, just once more.
It was as soft and sweet as the others had been,

she was too new for me to introduce her to more advanced play I know but I could hardly wait, I hope I survived it though, she seemed to have a natural affinity for the sensual.

She took to lovemaking as well as she did to kissing, her body was so welcoming, so thrilling, I could stay here like this forever.
I kissed her lips as I loved her, her small hands in the curve of my back pulling me closer let me know there was no discomfort. I kept a slow steady pace as her body trembled as I poured all my love and devotion into her.
Taking her into the bathroom I placed her in the now tepid water before I reheated it while adding bath salts to the soother I had already added to aid in any soreness she might suffer.

She still had a dreamy look on her face and I realized she had hardly said two words since she awakened, which was grounds for worry.
"Are you okay love?" I washed her hair as she reclined back against me, it wasn't the easiest thing to do in this position but I couldn't seem to get her to sit up she was completely boneless, I guess that's why I felt like I could lift the world

on my shoulders, nothing like satisfying a beautiful woman..

"Uh huh." She nodded her head and I was beginning to get worried it wasn't like my girl to be this quiet. If she didn't snap out of it the chief was going to know for sure that something was up. That's the last thing we needed; she'd probably kill him if he said anything.

I finally got her out of the tub and a little more awake, she was back to stealing kisses and rubbing herself against me, I wonder how that was going to change now that she knew where it led, we'll see. She seemed very taken with the whole making love thing and knowing her practice makes perfect attitude I'm sure we'd be spending lots of time behind closed doors, or out in the gardens, or in the pool or…shit I was making myself hard again. I had to leave her soon as I didn't want to be caught coming out of her rooms.

The chief, that fake was downstairs having a conversation with the dog who had snuck downstairs while we took our bath, it wasn't the first time I'd caught the two of them in a compromising position, they'd be hell to pay if Sam knew half the bad habits chief was teaching her pet.

"Well it took you two long enough to get down here, is it your new plan to starve me to death? You could've done that back home you didn't have to bring me all the way here to do me in."

"Shut it chief, Betty should have breakfast ready soon."

I'd let the staff return since I was going to be home for a while, I still had to figure out how we were going to handle the whole moving thing, but it will all work out. As long as I got them both here that's all I cared about right this minute.

"Miss. Priss what in the blazes is wrong with you?"

Oh no, please no, I knew that last time was too much she was walking as though she was in discomfort.

" Oh never mind, forget I said anything."
Apparently he had come to some conclusion on
his own, as long as it wasn't the right one I could
care less.
"Morning daddy."
"Morning da...what the blazes is wrong with you,
you get into the liquor again, that's it isn't it?"
"What is wrong with you chief she only said god
morning."

"She called me daddy, she hasn't used that
word since she was a preteen, but ever since she
turned into Regan MacNeil it's been either chief
or pop."
"Who the hell is Regan MacNeil?"
"Didn't you see the exorcist boy? Never fear, the
first time you get on Miss. Priss's bad side you'll
meet that little darling up close and personal. I've
had quite a few run-ins with her and let me tell
you it's not for the lily livered.
Thank God flower was too busy with her dog to
pay him any attention, then again she seemed
downright amiable today. If this is what kisses
and lovemaking did to her I was going to be sure
and keep her well supplied.

Chief

I think Miss. Priss, might be suffering from her womanly complaint, she's acting all funny and not right in the head, not that she ever was that, girl haven't been right since Adam was a lad.
At least she's not running me ragged, maybe the boy was good to have around after all, he seemed to have a calming effect on her, she did seem a bit dreamy this morning though.
I kept one eye peeled while I ate my nice breakfast of ham and eggs with home fried potatoes, she could be rather volatile around this time and you never knew from one minute to the next what might happen.

I tried getting clueless' attention but he was busy looking at the girl with a stupid look on his face. What a shame.
"Is this what the army is producing these days?"
Good that got his attention.
I rolled my eyes at him when he looked at me like

I was the one who had lost his mind.
"You're such a sap, before you know it you'll be running around here in an apron, it's pathetic."

I had to shake my head, I was looking for somebody to reel in Wild Bill but if the boy was gonna let her lead him around by the nose he won't be much help, looks like I'm gonna have to stick around here after all and keep these two outta trouble, she'd done gone and turned him into the village idiot, boy had a stupid ass grin on his face, now what the heck was that about I ask you? He'll learn soon enough when Miss. Priss beaned him with one of his fancy pots. Young people today, can't live with them can't send them to Devil's Island.

Chapter 33

GABE

It's been three days since I introduced Sam to the sins of the flesh, to say she was a quick study is putting it mildly, it took all my expertise as a covert operator to keep the goings on from the chief, let's just say my girl had no qualms about PDA, not that she was an exhibitionist or anything, she was just so innocent, and this was all so new, all she understood was that it felt good and she wanted it all the time.

At night behind closed doors she was a wild cat, during the day she cornered me for more of her kissing lessons, which were now steamier than ever, I did love her exuberance though I can't lie. I had her ring, which was perfect for her; it had been in my family for a good few generations, which meant it was old and romantic, from a time that my girl would appreciate.

204 | JORDAN SILVER

Right now she's crawled into my lap in the breakfast nook, no one else is around, Betty was off seeing to something else, she was just so happy to have someone else other than me to take care of these days, then again she could be playing cards with chief, that was their new thing.

"What the hell!" I jerked away from Samantha, just as she snarled. Looking over her shoulder I saw the culprit trying to escape in his wheelchair. He'd doused us in cold water. Well, he's only been threatening us with that for a few weeks now I guess it had finally gotten to be too much for him. I really shouldn't feel like laughing but my life was so good right now I don't think there was much that could get me down.

"You decrepit old coot, I'm gonna get you for that."
"Don't you threaten me Miss. Priss, you ought to see yourself, it's a crying shame, carrying on like that, you even scared the poor dog."
"Where's Charles, what did you do to him."
"Seen Fatal Attraction? Picture the rabbit." He laughed, the maniacal bastard, I'm sure my girl

had no idea what he was talking about thank God, all I needed was another world war on my hands.

See what I mean, from kisses to world wars in three seconds flat, never a dull moment.
"Picture a home for the infirm." My girl could give as good as she got.
"Listen, that stupid dog is hiding under my bed, I figured you two were in here getting up to your theatrics again and sent the poor dog into flight, a body can't walk around here these days without some type of carnal display smacking them in the face. Now if you two are through scaring the wild life around here, there's a little matter of getting back to Lexington. "
Sam huffed at him, good, my baby was in no more of a hurry to be separated from me than I was to be away from her.

I've been steadily talking her around to the marriage thing, no shamans needed thank you very much, just withhold kisses or an afternoon quickie and she was all ears, I still didn't understand what she had against marriage, but I was wearing her down.
"We'll talk about it later chief."
"Heard that before slick."

206 | JORDAN SILVER

"Po...op, what do we need to go back in such a hurry for?"

He looked at me and rolled his eyes.
"Uh, because we live there, and since you refuse to marry this reject I don't see why we should stay here."
"She said yes chief."
"It's about time, finally grew a pair did you G I Joe!"

I wonder how I could get away with tying him up somewhere for a few days, now his insults weren't just for my flower petal, more and more lately I've been feeling the blast from his tongue. "I'll let her at you I swear." That usually shut him the hell up, she hadn't tortured him much lately, she's been too busy with her new toy if you know what I mean, she's almost insatiable, and the way she wanted to learn everything was just...no words, nothing was forbidden it seemed, she was curious and generous and all kinds of wonderful, I couldn't wait till she was all mine.

SAM

Oh boy, oh boy, oh boy, if I thought I liked the kisses, well I like...that a whole lot. I get goose pimples just thinking about it. Okay I know we should be married first that's what all the books say, but I'm going to marry him anyway so it's okay.
I know I gave him a hard time about it, but this marriage thing is a big deal you know, what if he decides next year that he doesn't like me anymore, what will happen then? I asked him that very thing but he said if we didn't get married that he wouldn't keep doing those things to me because it would be disrespecting his friends' memory, his friend my brother Phil.

Besides if he changed his mind I'd just have to change it back for him, he didn't think I was leaving my gun in Lexington did he?
Anyway I really like it here and pop is looking healthier too even if he does complain like a

nattering old woman every chance he gets.

I can't believe he just threw water on us, he's been getting away with murder since we've been here, I've been trying to be good for Gabriel's family, didn't want them to suspect what a tyrant pop was, but this called for retribution, I don't have to think too hard about it, I know just where to get him.

Chief

Well it took the boy long enough, Rosemary's baby finally came around and agreed to marry him. I don't even want to know how he pulled it off. The kissing and carrying on was enough to make a body hurl, at least I knew the boy had good intentions, the way he looked at my kid, golden.

Yes indeed my Phil knew his mojo, these two were made for each other, the boy just needed to be a little more assertive though, he didn't know what he was getting into letting Miss. Priss run rough shod over him the way he did. Next thing you know she'd be running the roost and Lord help him then.
At least the kissing thing seemed to be coming along better, because I just threw cold water on Damien and there was no retaliation. Yes indeed things were coming along nicely, I can't wait for the actual wedding so she could become his headache and focus all her vengeance on him for a change. I'm sure that boy was going to live in the doghouse.

GABE

I wonder why the chief was looking at me like I was a sorry sight and shaking his head, who knows what went on inside that twisted head of his.

Chapter 34

GABE

Engaged. Yes! Though I had to use covert actions to bring it about.

We'd spent the night making love, or at least I tried making love to her, but she had other ideas. She liked me to be forceful with her when we were in bed I'd found and she had her own ways of getting what she wanted.

I just gave in to her, after all the end result is the same, and when I really wanted to be tender. I just was.

She was insatiable though and was learning her own tricks to get me going.

I wanted to do candle light and flowers when I proposed but that wouldn't work with my girl no, so I took matters in hand.

It's the morning after our marathon sexcapades,

I'm awake watching her sleep, waiting for her to awaken.

We usually tried to get up before chief stirred downstairs. He still didn't know that we were lovers.

She scrunched up her nose in that cute way she had of doing, it's how she wakes up every morning, then she did her stretch and smile bit, hands outstretched above her head.

It's when she brought them down again that her eyes popped open.

Her mouth dropped when she saw the size of the rock on her hand.

"You take that off, you throw me away."

"Gabriel..."

"No Samantha I'm serious you take that ring off that's it, I want you here with me but I will not live with you without marriage it's an insult to you and to your brother's memory.

She started to cry at the mention of Phillip. I pulled her to me kissing her hair and rubbing her shoulders." Don't cry baby he would be happy for us I know this with all my heart."

She nodded against my chest.

"It's going to be okay flower, there is nothing to

be afraid of okay!"
"Okay."

We spent some cuddle time while I got her all calmed down again.
Now she was admiring her ring.
"It's so pretty Gabriel."
"It's been in my family a very long time, I thought about buying you something new, but in the end I figured you would appreciate this one more."
The center stone was an emerald cut five carat with two stones on each side, I was extremely proud seeing it on her hand, knowing what it meant, that it was my seal of ownership; I'd become a barbarian in the last few weeks apparently, and she'd skin me if she new what I was thinking.

"It's perfect." She was smiling thank heaven I thought for sure there was gonna be a showdown.
"We need to get up, the chief will be up and about soon."
"A little longer, pleeeeaaase." She stole a kiss.
I knew where this was leading, what better way to seal our engagement.

"Okay, but we gotta be quick."

I had her flat on her back with her tongue in my mouth one hand cupping her breast while the other was between her legs. She was nice and warm and so fucking wet. I had to taste her before I entered her.

With her legs thrown over my shoulders I ate her to orgasm, which had her screaming and pulling my hair.

"Ride me baby."

I flipped over on my back pulling her over me and entered her hard and fast; she arched her back, nails digging into my chest as she set up her rhythm.

She loved to ride me, she liked the feeling of control it gave her, I watched the wonder on her face that was there each every time we came together like this.

Taking her hips in my hands I rocked forcefully up into her enjoying the tightness around me.

"Faster Gabriel, go faster."

Oh boy, she was in that kind of mood was she? Fine by me.

I pulled her off, turned her around on her hands

and knees and entered her from behind, now this is my favorite position.

"I'm gonna do you rough now okay baby!"

"Uh huh." That hitch in her voice was sexy as hell and the little gasp when I moved my cock inside her made my balls tingle.

I rocked into her nice and deep while holding onto her breasts, my chest against her back.

"You feel so good baby." My baby loved praise, especially when we were in bed, I loved the way it made her clench around me, the way her pussy milked me when I told her just what she meant to me.

I felt her pace quicken and her walls tighten around me as she pushed back to meet my thrusts; that was my cue so I grabbed onto her hips, leaned back and pounded to the finish.

Sam and Jenny have been gone for over two hours, they went shopping of all things, I was very surprised not to mention pleased when flower had been so excited about going shopping when she'd been so against it before though I didn't ask any questions just handed over my card and some additional funds which made her squeal and told her to have fun.

I would've felt much better if mom or even Darlene had gone with the but the driver would be along so that gave me a little comfort.

Chief and Prince Charles were around here somewhere, he'd already caused his quota of trouble for the day so I guess he was off regrouping.

He'd taken one look at Sam's hand and off he went.

"I guess you finally hogtied her huh!"

"Chief..."

"What, I'm just saying, how else did you get the rock of the dome on her hand?"

"It's the dome of the rock."

"Same thing."

I shook my head, why bother?
That had started the two of them bickering back
and forth, my baby was too happy to get too riled
though so his only punishment was dry wheat
toast for breakfast. Idiot.

The phone started ringing as he found me in
the den.
" Gabriel I'm so sorry."
"Jennifer what's going on, where is Samantha?" I
knew I shouldn't have let her leave without me.
" With...the police."

"WHAT?"
"There was a little problem could you please
come down to the station?"
I hung up the phone in a rush, my heart pumping
over time, what could possibly have happened?
Oh shit, this is flower we're talking about, Lord
please don't let anybody be dead.

"Let's go chief."
"Where we going?"

I really didn't want to tell him this, but there was no way around it.

"To the police station, seems your daughter was arrested."

"Good Lord, what did Oliver twist filch now?"

"Shame on you chief, I'm sure it's nothing like that, Sam would never do such a thing."

"I don't know what the country bumpkin would do when let loose in the city."

He was talking all that nonsense but I could tell he was very nervous.

"Don't worry chief whatever the hell's going on I'll get to the bottom of it.

We made it in ten minutes.

I walked swiftly inside to find Jennifer and Samantha handcuffed and sitting in some type of holding area.

This is after asking about six different people where to go.

Sam looked pissed and Jenny looked worried, and the officers looked harried.

"I'm Gabriel Sweeney, who do I talk to about getting these two out of here?"

The chief was giving his daughter looks like he was sorely put upon.

"Well sir, the lady wants to press charges but

we're waiting for the tale of the tape to see which way we should go since there seems to be a few differing opinions as to what really transpired."

"What lady?" What the hell was he talking about?
"It was Brenda Gabriel she found us in the store and followed us around pestering poor Sam.
We tried to get away from her but she wouldn't let up, we even went to the dressing room to get away from her but she followed us there too;
then she started calling Sam names and she got in her face..."

"Yep, that's a sure fired way to get Rocky Balboa ramped up, guess she didn't learn her lesson the first time around eh champ?"
I didn't even bother shushing him, what was the damn point? My life used to be so peaceful: yeah but I wouldn't change it for anything.
"Well, then Sam...she..."
The cop decided to pick it up from there.

"Apparently Miss. Holder tried to choke the life out of Miss. Winters."

"Way to go Albert De Salvo."

"Chief shut it."

"Okay so what do we need to do now to get her out of here, besides this tape business, should I be contacting my lawyers?"

"Not quite, like we said our guys are going over the tape to see if their story can be corroborated, if so then they're free to go. If not we'll have to book them and then you can call your lawyers."

I looked over at Sam who still hadn't said anything which was not at all normal, she did look royally pissed though. I decided to leave well enough alone and wait until we got home.

"What did you do to her, why is she so quiet?"

"She's quiet now sir, but...is she a law student perchance?"

"No why do you ask?"

"Well she sure does know a lot about the law."

"Her father was chief of police back home."

"Heard about him too, yes sir, we got an earful, that's why we're going through the tape now as opposed to waiting. You're the fiance I take it, the one who would skin us alive if we touched a hair on her head!"

"That would be me yes, no one touched her did they?" I think I heard the older of the two mutter 'who would risk it?'
Damn straight.

"Why were you arrested Jenny?"
"Honestly, I don't know, I was trying to get Sam off the blonde idiot and she started screeching that we were trying to kill her, so I belted her one to get her to shut the hell up."
"Stupid waste of space."
"Uh oh, Sweeney Todd has decided to speak."
I'm gonna lock chief in a cell and leave him here, either that or let Sam make good on one of her threats and bean him with something if he didn't shut up.
Of course my parents showed up, Jenny was still a minor after all.

When they had been appraised of the situation they were none too pleased to say the least.
"That's it for the Winters son, I don't care what dealings you have with them, that's it, to have not only my daughter but my new daughter in law arrested as well, there are no words."

"Yes mom."

She meant that shit too, she saw nothing wrong with dissolving contracts that were worth millions not to mention the headache of severing business alliances, and truth be known neither did I.

If they couldn't keep a leash on their daughter, or sister, whatever relation she was to them, then I had no uses for them.

I went over and kissed my baby since she was no longer looking like she was ready to chew nails. The chief was pestering the poor officers about who knows what, probably sharing old war stories.

"You okay there sweetheart?" Dumb question I know, but I had no idea what to say when the love of your life was arrested.

"I'm fine, I just wish that hussy would leave me alone, she's worst than Diana and Paula combined, jeez. Next time I'm bringing my gun, nobody listens to me unless I'm peppering their backside with buckshot."

"I'm thinking you might not want to say that too loud around here."

"Ooh, good one, sorry, where's my baby?"
"I left him home with Betty."
"You know pop's never gonna let me live this down right?"
"I'll keep him in line flower, don't worry about it."
She seemed more worried about that than the outcome of this fracas.

At the end of the day the tale of the tape freed the two girls and the tables were turned. When Sam was asked if she wanted to press charges for harassment mom took that bull by the horns and said yes.
Oh Lord now she was on the warpath, that's all I needed.
We left the station house and headed home, of course chief couldn't leave well enough alone.

"So tell me there my Bostonian friend, how does it feel to be a criminal?"
"She's not a criminal chief, she wasn't even really arrested."
I tried to head shit off before he got her going, it was never a good idea while driving to let those two go at each other.
"They put the steel on her, she was two minutes

away from the clinker, CRI- MI-NAL."

"Chief, what did you have for breakfast this morning, and dinner a few nights ago, do you never learn?"
She was still messing with his food when he pissed her off, which turned my house into an enemy camp, but still he persisted in starting shit with her.
"I'm not afraid of Miss. Priss, her new best friends and I have an understanding, she starts anything with me I have their numbers, us cops stick together you know."

"You know pop I've been thinking."
Oh shit.
"You know how you're afraid of kittens..."
He started sputtering after that, I was laughing my ass off, the chief was afraid of kittens?

Chief

Engaged and arrested all on the same day, only Calamity Jane, I don't know what I'm gonna do with that girl. Thank the heavens she wouldn't be my problem much longer, the boy had put a rock the size of Jupiter on her finger.
My little girl, I could just cry I was so happy, but she had already put my manhood in question with that crack about kittens. I wonder how she had figured it out anyway: when she was younger every time she would ask for one I would tell her I was allergic, I wonder when she figured out the truth? Those things scared the crap outta me.

Chapter 35

GABE

I just put the chief and Sam on my private plane to return to Lexington without me, it felt like tearing off my right arm. They were with me for almost three months but it felt like two weeks. I wanted them to stay but they had to return to see about closing up their home and getting things in order, of course I wanted to go with them but business matters kept me from making the trip. I felt like half a person as I made my way to the office, her sad little face wreaking havoc with my heart.

Of course the chief had rolled his eyes and mumbled about face sucking and what a disgrace we were, but he was a little sad himself. I would be meeting them in a couple weeks to bring them home, at least that was a happy thought, but how the hell was I supposed to live without her for that long? Even the chief was going to be missed.

The damn mausoleum was going to feel empty without them, there now I'm insulting my own home, I've become just as warped as he is.

228 | JORDAN SILVER

It's been two days and I've spent about ten of the forty-eight hours they've been gone on the phone with her. I got her the iPhone, an iPad and a MacBook but she still just calls me, no FaceTime for my girl, I really need to drag her into the twenty first century like the chief keeps saying. My phone rang and their house number showed up, did she lose her phone already?
"Baby?"

"Baby? Baby? don't baby me you snake."
"Chief?"
"Exactly what the hell was going on up those stairs while you had me locked away in the basement?"
"Basement, what the hell..." Had chief finally lost his ever loving mind? I knew this day was coming but not this soon.
"Listen here Lothario, Sam's been sick every morning since we've been here, I only just put two and two together, because... well never mind that..."

"Sick, what do you mean sick, she was fine when she left here."
"Boy, shut your yap and listen, she's sick as a dog when she wakes up, then about an hour later she's

buzzing around here like a worker bee, and the only thing she doesn't eat is the wood off the table..."
"Sick how chief, I'm not understanding you."
"Lord help my poor grandchildren, some people should not be allowed to reproduce."
"Chief!"

"Boy read between the lines, she throws up every morning like clockwork, then an hour or so later she's fit as a fiddle and starving like a pack of hyenas on a buffalo's ass what do you think that means?"
I had to give it some thought, but I got it eventually, especially after all the mutterings about brain dead baby fathers who didn't have the sense God gave a duck.
"Oh shit..."

"Exactly, now your problem is who's going to tell the clueless wonder that is my daughter? Because she actually thinks she has a stomach bug. I'm not telling her cause who knows how she'll react to the news so that's on you. Now listen here J Edgar, when you tell her please leave me out of it, and I don't mean like the last time when you blabbed and got me in trouble, this is your mess you fix it on your own thank you very much. And when you're done it's you and me in the back yard for some fisticuffs."

"Uh, chief, I'm not fighting you."
I had a stupid grin on my face, my baby was having our baby.
"Whatever, two things, you better tell Summer and Jenny to get that wedding ball rolling or better yet head to the justice of the peace, and two you better get here quick before Jane does her Tarzan and Jane stuff with Brand, jumping off cliffs."
"What the hell?"
"Oh she didn't tell you, that's one of their favorite pastimes, jumping off the cliffs at the state park a few towns over, se ya."

Chief

I'm too old for this mess, between those two I'll be raising this kid on my own, I'm already raising the damn dog. Miss. Priss don't know spit about no dog, damn thing's been sissified.
I wasn't too bent out of shape about the baby, not really, these young people today are so hot blooded what can you do? Besides the boy was marrying her wasn't he? I just had to keep her from doing something crazy before he was able to tell her what was going on, the girl really had no clue, I guess no woman in the house was to blame for that. The stomach flu.

Oh spit, I hope she wasn't bringing in a ringer, that's all I need another one of her running around to make me nuts.
Maybe I ought to move in with Geoffrey save myself the aggravation.
Then again no, if I want my grand kid to have a lick a sense I was gonna have to be there to see he or she was raised right, obviously there was no hope for Pippy Longstocking, but another little girl might be nice to raise. Lord help us all.

Gabe

I called up the pilot to schedule a flight plan and get the plane ready, it's funny how a week ago business matters kept me here, now those same matters seemed so insignificant. I had called the chief to let him know I was on my way, he'd grumbled something about tying her down until I got there. I hope for his sake he was kidding, she's likely to bean him with something if he tried. Hopefully I'll get there in time before all the theatrics.

A baby, I can't believe it, what if chief was wrong and it really was just a bug? No, we hadn't once used protection, was that my subconscious way of tying her to me? Or was it just that every time I got her naked my common sense went out the window and all I could think about was being inside her? Better think of something else there Sweeney you have a long flight ahead of you.

Chief

I hope that boy hurries up and get here this child is like to put me in an early grave. After this mornings' ode to the throne, which is when I called the baby daddy. Lord my daughter was pregnant out of wedlock...never mind that now, anyway ever since then she's been on a tear. Her and that stupid dog have been running around here cleaning and spraying and who knows what. I'm not sure all this excitement was good for the baby, but what did I know? And since she didn't know she was knocked up, and I had no intentions on being the one to inform her, I was gonna have to come up with something to keep her quiet for the rest of the day.

"Oh, ugh..."
"Pop?" She came running into the living room; okay that wasn't so good either, but hey. ,
"What's the matter with you, you sick, you hurt yourself?"
I rolled my eyes where she couldn't see at least it had worked.

"I don't feel so good Priss, I think I need to go to the hospital or something." Lord let her talk me out of this.
"Why, what's wrong?"
I just feel...off."
"Off how?"

Good Lord was she gonna talk me to death? Maybe I should've thought this thing through better.
"Off, off, what do you mean off how?"
"What hurts, you been in the whiskey again?"
"Excuse me, there's only one lush in this family and it so happens to be you, thank you very much."

"I guess you're okay since your lips are still flapping."
Damn me and my big mouth: what to do now?
"Maybe I'm allergic to the flying squirrel."
"You can move out he's staying."
She kissed the ugly thing after that atrocious statement, oh it's on now; this is the thanks I get for trying to save her skin.
"Listen you…"

GABE

I got there as soon as I could from the airport and from the looks of things I'd made it just in time, there appeared to be some sort of standoff underfoot in the Holder residence. It had only been a week, but I had missed this, in fact it was getting harder to remember my life before them. You and that mutt can both go...."

"Ahem, hello chief." I couldn't have him tormenting my pregnant fiancee now could I? "Gabriel..." My word but that smile alone was worth the trip. She flew into my arms, lurched, grabbed her stomach, covered her mouth and ran for the restroom. Shit, until that moment it hadn't really registered, hadn't quite sunk in this was for real. One look at the chief and I knew for sure it was. His eyes were working overtime.

"Might as well strap something around her neck as often as she does that."
"Chief, a little compassion please."
"You didn't hear what she said to me before you showed up."

"I'm sure you didn't instigate any of it right."
"I was trying to keep her in the house until you got here, the girl is liable to be jumping off a cliff or riding a motorcycle at break neck speeds."

"Oh Gabriel, you came all this way and now you're gonna get sick, you can't come near me, I think I caught something and now I think that one is catching it too." She pointed at her father when she said this.

"That one, that's how you address your father, and it will be a complete miracle not to mention disaster if I had what you have. In fact I think it's still impossible, no matter how far man has come with science and technology.
"Chief!"
He huffed and piped down, I 'm not sure she understood his ramblings, but just in case, that was no way for her to learn she was going to be a mother.

"Sam baby let's go sit and talk, you won't make me sick I promise." She still looked skeptical but went ahead of me to sit on the couch. "Dumber than a bag a hammers." I actually flicked his ear for that one, even though he mumbled it: it was still loud enough to hear.

"I see you miss baby food, why don't you leave well enough alone before she really clobbers you?"

"Humph, and you think that would be the first time, think again, that termagant is always being violent, and me being an invalid."

"Parsnips, kale, turnips, sound good for dinner pop?"

He blanched and sputtered as I shook my head and followed after her. He'll never learn.

I sat next to her on the couch and took both her hands in mine.

"Do you know why I'm here flower?" She shrugged her shoulders.

"You finished your stuff early so you came?" I shook my head and kissed her hair, I couldn't resist.

"No, your father called me, he said you weren't feeling too well."

"He did, why would he bother you about that? It's just a little bug, no big deal."

I could hear the chief who was eavesdropping from the doorway huffing and muttering. No doubt I was gonna hear all about using his name and getting him involved before

238 | JORDAN SILVER

too long. How else he thought I should explain my presence to her was beyond me.

"The reason I'm here is because..." Shit, how to proceed? This could go either way, she could either be excited about the baby, or she could totally flip out. I'm hoping for the former.
"We think you might be pregnant Sam." There, I said it nice and quick, maybe that'll soften the blow. She squinted at me, looked down at her tummy, looked back at me and shook her head no.

I nodded mine yes, she pulled her shirt up and looked at her stomach. I almost laughed, it was as though she expected to see evidence of the baby right away.
"Good God girl fix yourself, that's how you got into this predicament in the first place I bet. Good Lord tell me my grand baby wasn't conceived during her alcohol fuse, child will probably be born with a bottle in it's hand."

In that moment I realized something. This was his way of protecting her, whenever he thought something was going to be too much for her to process or was going to upset her, he tried to distract her by being difficult.

It always seemed to work too; good job chief, I looked over and smiled at him, he saw the understanding on my face, I saw the anxiety on his.

"But Gabriel..."
"Yes baby?" She was whispering so I followed suit, I guess this wasn't for the chief's ears.
"We didn't do all that stuff you're supposed to do, to you know..."
I was lost, what the hell did she mean? She couldn't have forgotten all those times I took her to my bed or joined her in hers could she?
"Flower, you do remember that we made love don't you?"

"Sssh." She looked back at her father who was rolling his eyes and muttering under his breath, I wonder if he realized he was petting the dog, his supposed archenemy.
"Of course I remember, I'm not a complete ninny but we didn't do the other stuff."
Huh, lord help me what was going on in that head of hers now?
"What other stuff baby?"

"You know, I didn't put my legs up...after, or any of that other stuff that they say you have to do when you want to have a baby."

There was a choking sound coming from the doorway; I sent him a glare to keep him quiet this was a delicate situation after all.
"Baby, some women only do that in certain situations, didn't you study any of this stuff in your homeschooling?"
"Kinda but...and you think there's a baby in there?"
She pointed to her stomach, I nodded, and the sun came out.
Oh thank God.
I smiled over at the chief who took a deep breath; she was going to be okay.

She had the most radiant smile on her face then she started to laugh.
"Pop, guess what."
"What Priss?" He was smiling now too.
"You can't catch what I got." She thought that was hilarious.
"You hoo, Holder family."
Uh oh, that sounded like those girls, what now?

"Wasn't me, I didn't invite anybody." Chief put his hands up in surrender, I could see flower already building up a good head of steam. Those girls really did rub her the wrong way, but then she did the strangest thing, she started smiling and playing with her ring, and if I hadn't seen it with my own two eyes I would never have believed it. She lounged back against the back of the couch draping her hand across to show her ring to the best advantage.

"Paula, Diana, how nice to see you, won't you join us?"
Of course the hand was swinging from left to right with every word and you would have to be blind not to see the rays that came off the rock from the reflection of the sunlight coming through the windows.
"Oh my...Samantha are you engaged?"

I think that was Diana speaking but I'm not too sure, whenever I had been in their presence I hadn't had enough time to get to know who was who before my flower was running them off.
"Yes I am."
"To who?" They both looked around the room as though expecting to see some mystery man.

"To Gabriel of course."

Uh oh she sounded a little peeved, I looked over at the chief who had a half grin on his face he did like a good show after all.
The stupid girl took her life in her hands and started laughing.
"Oh shit." You got that right chief.
"Good one Sam, no seriously who is it? It's not that Brandon is it? I mean I know your options are limited but even you can do better than that: let me see, is the ring even real?"

I was about to step in but even I had to admit that was a low blow, chief looked ready to chew off his tongue, I decided to sit back and let my girl do her thing. Brandon indeed.
"You know me girls, always the joker, why don't I get you two something nice and cold to drink?"
Uh huh, kitchen around here equals shotguns; I should probably put a stop to this, but what the hell. The chief didn't even try.

I wondered how these two couldn't hear all the muttering and stomping around in there.
"Flower no stomping love remember, we have to be careful now."
"Oh, oh yeah I forgot, don't mind me Gabriel."

"So Gabriel back so soon?"
I don't know which one she was but she started winking her eyes at me just before all hell broke loose.

"Not good enough for a man like Gabriel am I?" That's all she said before she really took a shot at them, right down the middle.
Prince Charles yelped and jumped off of chief's lap and headed for cover, smart dog. Chief was laughing like a loon and I had finally gotten my head out of my ass and was trying to get the gun away from flower.

"Okay baby that's enough."
The two clueless ninnies as Sam would say were ducking and hiding behind the love seat.
"That's it, that's the last time we try to be friends with you, you, you...unghhh." They stomped out the door keeping a weary eye on her the whole time.
"Good riddance to bad rubbish."

I had my hand around her middle to keep her from going after them, she was a blood thirsty little thing when riled no doubt about it.
"Settle down baby, remember, you can't be getting so excited anymore, it can't be good for the baby."

I kissed her hair as she softened.

"Listen here Annie Oakley, you put that damn gun down and act like you got some sense. I think it's time we hurried this moving business along before the law shows up to cart you off. What the hell do you read in those books of yours anyway? I thought those Brits were a peace loving bunch, where you get all this fire and piss from is beyond me."

"I have to go shopping." I was getting whiplash dealing with her moods today, then again what was new about that?
"What do you need baby?"
"Pregnant clothes of course." She smiled wide at me, I couldn't help it, I kissed the hell out of her, why burst her bubble and tell her that it was going to be a while before she needed that stuff?

"Lord help us, she's really gone off the deep end this time."
"Chief!"
"Maternity clothes and this morning she didn't even know she was pregnant, I don't know where I went wrong."

He went off muttering to himself as usual while I stole some more kisses. One more disaster averted, whew.

Chapter 37

Chief

Guess where I am, go ahead, I bet you in a thousand years you'd never guess. Why? because rational people with common sense don't think like my little family. Obviously what my Phil saw in these two was that they were both cracked. My daughter who hasn't gained an ounce since she was fifteen is at the mall, thank the good Lord it's in Annandale and not the little mall we have back in Lexington or I would die of embarrassment on the spot.

What's she doing here you ask? Well I'll tell you, maternity clothes, yes you heard me right, Miss. Priss and the clueless wonder that she's about to marry in a couple months dragged me off to the mall to buy her fat clothes, never seen anything like it in all my days.

"I don't see why I had to be here, you should just order her a gunnysack, the way she's been eating since she heard those magical words, you're gonna need it."

"Would you be quiet? Let her enjoy this she's having fun."

"Son...I never thought I'd day this to a fighting man, but I'm embarrassed to know you."

"Yeah, why's that?" Not that I cared, whatever came out of his mouth it was bound to be contrary.

"You couldn't tell her that this was stupid? The girl is skinny as a rail, where's she going in fat clothes?"

"First of all you cranky old geezer, they're not fat clothes and you better not let her hear you calling them that or you're on your own when she goes after you again. I've been here a week and a half and I've had to save your hide at least three times already."

"You didn't stop her this morning when she popped me one behind the head." Damn infuriating girl, I just knew she was going to be even more of a pain than usual, what with hormones and what not.

"You called her an imbecilic ingrate, whatever the heck that means. You're lucky that's all she did, and I did save you, I started kissing her to take her mind off of you didn't I?"

"And that's another thing, if you want me to move in with you two you're gonna have to take it easy on the tonsil hockey." He started laughing like a loon.

"What the hell is so funny? You think I'm kidding but you two are a public nuisance, a body can't turn around without being assaulted by your fornicating."

"Chief!"

"Whaaaat?"

"Shut it, here she comes be nice, I don't care what you really think, just say it looks nice or I'll get her a kitten on the way home."

"You...traitor to the male species, turn in your man card Sweeney, cause you're not using it that I can see."

"Whatever, you just be nice to my flower or you're gonna get it."

GABE

These two, sheesh, nonstop comedy from one day to the next, I could barely keep up. I had taken Sam to a doctor in Annandale the day after I arrived and had had the news confirmed. To say we were both excited would be a vast understatement, I was over the moon, and I don't think my flower has come down yet. I was able to put her off from this shopping trip for a few days since we still had a lot to do to get ready for the move, all I had to do was remind her that we would be going home soon, the quicker they got things sorted out.

I had to let mom in on the secret since the wedding had to be moved up, you can imagine the screaming and yelling that ensued. Mom was excited about her first grandchild, but flustered as to how she was going to move up the wedding of the century on such short notice. Apparently it was a pretty small task for her since she'd called me back the next day with the news that everything would be ready in two months. We're getting married fuck yeah, this morning my baby put her foot down, she was tired of packing and sorting, she wanted to go shopping.

Chief who could never leave well enough alone started calling her insulting names because she had no tummy as yet but was in an all fired hurry to wear fat clothes as he so eloquently put it. She sure was cute though she was always walking around the house with one hand covering her tummy and a smile on her face. I've had to glare the chief into quietness more than once to keep him from tormenting her.

Everything out of her mouth was about the baby these days, what would we name it, did I want a boy or a girl did I think she would be a good mother? And the reason why I had stayed and will stay with her business be damned, will she end up like her mom? That one broke my heart, as excited as she was she was a little afraid as well, afraid that she would die in childbirth as her mother had.

I'd watched the chief one night during their nightly ritual as he calmed her fears, reminding her that her mom had had Phil with no problem and that it wasn't because of her that her mom had passed, but because of her weak heart. I'd gone up to her bed with tears in my eyes. When she came up later that night I had lifted her in my arms and taken her to Phil's room, I remembered that the chief was right under her room, I didn't need any of his rhetoric in the morning.
I made sweet, tender love to her all through the night until her mind was filled with nothing but me.

Now here we are in the store trying on clothes and she was beaming. She's wearing this blue colored dress with a high waist that flowed down to her knees. It was short and sassy and looked like a dress any teenage girl would wear, at least that's what it looked like to me.

"What do you think, is it nice?" She twirled around in front of us.
"I think it looks beautiful baby."
"That doesn't look like fat clothes at all, looks pretty normal to me, you might want to get it in a size up though cause the way you've been putting

252 | JORDAN SILVER

it away lately that's not gonna make it pass next
month."

Lord, why me, why can't I be the type of
guy to let her finish him?
"Samantha don't do it, no fast movements
remember? that's a good girl." She was about to
swing on him, in the store, with witnesses.
She mumbled something and gave him the death
glare, while the idiot laughed his head off, of
course I knew my girl wouldn't let him get the
best of her.
"Hey pop...meow." And with that she turned and
walked back towards the fitting room.
He looked at me as if seeking help I just shook my
head and walked away. He'll never learn.

Chapter 38

Chief

Well, it's that day, wedding day. I'm hanging around outside the dressing room where my little girl is being primped and buffed for her big day, I hope they removed all sharp objects from the room before hand. All the girls are in there and through the door it sounds like a gaggle of hens clucking away at each other. Darlene and Summer are in there with the stylists and Lord knows who else.

Now I'm sure everyone thinks I'm hanging around because I'm nervous, they'd be wrong, I'm hanging around because....well have you seen runaway bride? Uh huh, with my kid who knows what might happen, I'm not taking any chances, the sooner he claps that ring on her finger, the sooner I can breathe easy and my worrying will be over for at least the next six or seven months until my grand baby comes along. I already know I'm going to be the one raising the kid, with these two as parents how can I not?

Poor Sweeney's gonna have his hands full with Miss. Priss alone, speaking of which, I have to remember to have a talk with Summer and Caleb, get them on board the grandparent's band wagon, I'm not sure they're as aware as I am of our offspring's cuckooness, poor kid will be running around shooting at stuff by the time he or she's four, and the way that boy doted on my girl I could just imagine his little ones would have him wrapped around their little fingers, which meant they'd be wreaking havoc and causing mayhem wherever they went.

Nope, I owed it to the greater Richmond area to curtail that mess before it got off the ground.

GABE

My flower looks amazing as she walks towards me down the aisle. I released the breath I had been holding all morning, with my Sam you just never knew which way the wind would blow. I'd spent the better part of last night reassuring her father that everything will be fine. He seemed to think that she might make a run for it. According to him you never knew what notion she would get in her head from one minute to the next. He soon had me convinced I should be worried.

I'd stayed in the guesthouse last night because tradition said I shouldn't see her before today; sometime around two in the morning her warm body had joined me in my bed. We didn't exchange a word, I just folded her body under mine and held her close. I held my two babies close throughout the night until the early hours of the morning when I made slow passionate love to her before walking her back over before the others awakened.

Now here we are, she's walking towards me to become mine completely, her smile letting me know that she was okay, not nervous, no second thoughts, nothing. Chief wheeled his chair next to her until they reached me, before anyone could do or say anything flower reached up on her toes and kissed my lips. The guests laughed and I smiled at her to let her know it was okay, she didn't seem too worried about it though.
Chief of course was rolling his eyes but I ignored him.

"Lord love a duck...." I think I heard him mumble that before heading to his place with my family. Since it was just him we decided he would stay on my side, we were all one family now. The last couple weeks have been wonderful, and I'm hoping they were a precursor to our life to come. There's been lots of laughter and planning, the only cloud on our otherwise unblemished horizon was the fact that Philip couldn't be here. I'd solved that melancholy mood by doing shots with chief while we exchanged old war stories and later, loving flower into exhaustion.

Her appetite for any and all things sexual seems to have amplified with pregnancy, at least that's what I think is causing this astronomical change in her. I'm lucky if I get out of bed before eight in the mornings now, where before I would be up and ready by six. Being an early riser herself we have kind of a routine going. It usually started with flower rolling over with a groan before hotfooting it to the bathroom, where I would hold her hair and wipe her face until her sickness had passed. Then I would get her an ice - cold ginger ale, which we now kept stocked in a mini fridge in the bedroom because it seemed to be the only thing that helped with the nausea.

After this production, which lasted all of ten or fifteen minutes on a bad day, she'd crawl back into bed after we both brushed our teeth, dragging me with her. Then the fun begins, we always started out slow, soft touches, secret murmurs, my hands gliding all over her body especially at the heat between her thighs. She'd be hot and ready for me, I'd kiss her until she drew me over and into her, rocking our pelvises together in a nice slow dance, our tongues mating as her warmth coddled me deep.

We'd come together like that, held tightly in each others arms the way we always did, but that's where it changed, because no sooner would I have caught my breath than my flower would be taking me into her mouth bringing me back to life again. Now don't get me wrong, I like it, it's just...strange. Sam for all her theatrics can be a bit of a prude; her ideals can sometimes be Victorian to say the least. Our first few months of lovemaking were quite tame, nothing to complain about mind you, I was very satisfied with our encounters, and would've stayed that way for the rest of our lives.

There was passion, love, so much love, and honestly, I didn't see anything lacking when we came together, I guess the problem is I never expected to, well...fuck Samantha, you see, there is a difference, our first session in the morning, that was lovemaking, what we did the second and sometimes third time, that was something else entirely and it was all initiated by her.

She'd start by taking me into her mouth, her juices still fresh on my shaft, she'd lick and suck and nip me back to erection, all the while laughing and teasing, fascinated with that part of me that brought her so much pleasure, then she'd climb aboard and ride me, her hands clasping mine to her breasts which she loved for me to knead. It wouldn't be long before she was cumming again, then she'd pull off, get on her hands and knees beside me and wiggle her fine ass until I got up behind her.

It was a well-choreographed dance. "Harder Gabriel, please." And with that there would be a wild romp to the finish. No matter how hard I pounded or how deep I went, it never seemed hard or deep enough. She wasn't a talker she let her body do the talking for her, after urging me to go harder or faster, she'd use the walls of her sex to control me, by that I mean taking all control away from me. The pleasure was twofold, my trigger being not only the pulsations of her sex around me, but the knowledge that my child was inside her, it always made me cum harder than ever before.

I was jolted back to the present by Flower's softly spoken 'I do.' Damn, no one warned me what those two little words could do, the overwhelming feelings that would overcome me in that moment when she pledged herself to me for all eternity, that was no small thing, not to me and not to her. I looked to the chief after the kissing of the bride and with a slight nod and clasping her arm between my elbow and my side, the baton was passed. I accepted the challenge, I'd kept my promise.

Epilogue

Chief

Lord love a duck, Miss. Priss is about to pop any minute now, anybody with an ounce of sense can see that, but do these two listen to me, of course not.

I knew that boy wasn't going to be any help when it came to reining her in, in fact she was worse now than she ever was, why, because he coddled her something awful it was a crying shame.

Like now, all I can do is shake my head at the two of them.

"I thought the turkey was supposed to be stuffed or are we having duck?

"Chief!"

I wish the boy would stop calling my name like that: truth is my girl did favor a stuffed turkey and from behind she waddled like a duck. The only one too chicken to admit it was her husband who kept telling her how beautiful she was which he had to do every ten minutes because she cried at the drop of a hat these days. It was getting so I couldn't even watch TV with her any more because she would cry at every blessed thing, I didn't know coffee was a reason for tears but what do I know? When I told her to stop being a weeping willow she tried to brain me and that husband of hers had the nerve to take her side, like that's new.

Now he was taking offense because I was once again speaking the truth, the girl was big as a mansion.
"Is she having a litter, because I don't think I've ever seen a human female that big before."
"Sssh, it's okay baby, he's just teasing, you're gorgeous I promise." He whispered something in her ear that made her all sappy again.

I rolled my eyes because that's all that went on around here these days it was enough to make a body ill; ever since they came back from their honeymoon it's been the same, moony eyes and simpering. Hah.
"What time are the others getting back? I wanna show Geoffrey and Brand my new fishing rods."
"Pop you said you didn't want to go with Caleb and Summer, but Geoffrey and Brand could go;

now every five minutes you're asking when they'll be back."

"And how pray tell is that bothering you, huh? Why don't you have another marshmallow with peanut butter?" I couldn't help it if I turned my nose up at that, I mean just the sound of it was disgusting.

"Sam baby, remember that nice Siamese cat that the lady said she was going to find for you? Well I'm gonna check with her today see if anything came in."

He had the nerve to look at me all smug when he said it too, traitor.

"Why don't you hand over your man card while you're at it, sap?" I whispered as he came near.

"You keep messing with my wife I'll get her three cats, besides you stole her dog so it's only fair she should get her kittens."

"I did not steal that flea infested vermin, you two left him here for three weeks while you went gallivanting all over who knows where and he clung on to me, poor thing, what was I to do, tune him out?"

Stupid dog kept following me around everywhere now, Miss. Priss was none too happy that I'd spoilt her dog but what did she expect? The dog was dumb.

"What does she need with a cat anyway? She's about to pop any second and who's gonna watch after some fool cat."
He grinned like the fool he is so I ignored him. He wasn't too bad all things considered, he'd fixed up my own wing downstairs and made everything accessible for me, his new thing was packing me off to Switzerland of all places because some quack over there swears he can fix what's wrong with my kickers, whatever, we'll see, I told the boy not to waste his money but of course he had to go set Annie Wilkes on me.

Now I was booked for travel right after the holidays with Geoffrey in tow, that's the kind of things my son in law did. The only reason I finally agreed was because I wanted to run after my grand baby.

Any way today is turkey day and like I was saying, I don't know who's more stuffed, Sam or the bird.
"Why isn't Betty cooking thanksgiving dinner?"

"Because Betty has a family and I wanted her to have the time off to be with them, now stop complaining and come help pop."
"Help with what? you're eating more stuffing than is going into the bird, they're going to be some hungry people at that dinner table tonight that's for sure."

I was barely in time to duck the wooden spoon full of stuffing that came flying at my head but not quick enough to avoid the shoe. She clocked me but good in the old noggin.
"Did you see that? she beaned me, such violence and against your helpless old man."
"Samantha, stop it."
Oh so he decided to jump in after the damage was done.
"Chief stop teasing her, go play with prince Charles or find something to do."
"I'm bored how long does it take to buy this special whatever it is that Miss. Priss just have to have anyway?"

GABE

Pure bliss, that's what my life has become, my little flower is in the words of her aggravating father 'big as a mansion' but what a beautiful mansion. She glows, I know people say that all the time, but when it comes to my Sam, it's absolutely true.
I wasn't too sure about her fixing thanksgiving dinner for everyone though but she insisted she was fine to do it, our baby was due any day now and I couldn't wait.

The nursery was already set up and no matter all his posturing and grumbling the chief was about as excited as we were.
They still had their late night talks where she laid her head against his knee and he brushed her hair, I don't think anyone else knew about that but me though, the way they went at each other the rest of the day no one would believe me anyway.

She's bopping around the kitchen in something she calls Juicy Couture, all I know is that her little round belly, okay not so little and

her beautifully rounded ass look amazing in the
dark blue suit.
Only Samantha would wear sapphires and
diamonds with a track suit and make it look hot.
I better stop giving her hungry looks before chief
catches on and makes some remark that would get
him killed, fool.

He still hadn't learned not to mess with her
yet, and pregnancy hasn't slowed her down much,
she still manages to brain him at least once a week
on average.
The honeymoon had been amazing, though we
hardly saw much of our surroundings, it was the
first time we'd ever been completely alone and
we'd been sure to repeat that a time or two since
our return.

Flower was very...innovative and she was
rather playful in bed. The doctor said it was okay
to make love to her up until the end of her
pregnancy, I wish he'd told her that her poor
husband was still just a man and not a machine.
She had an even more voracious appetite.

As chief left the kitchen grumbling under his
breath I walked back over to her.
"I have something to show you in the bedroom."

She started blushing immediately because she knew what those words meant.

"Gabriel, the others will be back soon."

"I only need ten minutes, I promise." I put her hand on my hardening shaft and rubbed it up and down. She added a little squeeze, which made me groan out loud.

Grabbing her hand in mine, I turned down the stove and headed up the back stairs to our room.

Behind closed doors I pulled down her pants and panties, bent her over the bed and down on my knees I ate her sweet little pussy from behind, holding her open with my fingers.

She was already wet and aching I could tell because she kept trying to rub her legs together. Standing behind her, I rubbed my cock head up and down from the crack of her ass to her clit, stopping to tease her slit.

She widened her legs trying to draw me in.

With her hard lower stomach held safely in my hand I used the other to guide my cock into her.

"Umm...." All the way in, fuck that felt amazing, she was like a furnace inside.

"Please touch my breasts, they hurt."

I reached for both tits, kneading gently as I rocked back and forth trying not to go too deep too fast.
"You feel amazing baby, and your ass is beautiful, I want to bite it."
She squeezed down on me and juiced at my words of praise.

"Go faster Gabriel, please, faster."
"Ssh, ssh, nice and easy baby."
She clenched the sheets in her fists and pushed back on my cock.
"Sam....." I said in warning.
"No, go faster, I need it faster."
She touched her clit letting me know she was close.

I watched as my cock slid in and out of her, what an erotic sight, and the wet sound of her pussy around my cock turned me on even more.
"I love being inside you, so beautiful."
I sped up my thrusts as she throbbed and spasm all over me.
When I came I had to check my thrusts as my body wanted to pound wildly, buried to the hilt in her I exploded.

"Dinner was amazing Samantha, my gosh I can't believe you did all this yourself."

"Thanks Summer, but Gabriel helped."

"Child I know my son is helpless in the kitchen."

"Thanks mom."

Sam went to get up I'm sure to clear plates, which was not going to happen but as she stood, she stopped short and breathed out heavily.

"Gabriel..." She looked at me with tears in her eyes.

"Oh shit." I was around the table and at her side in a flash, pulling her chair back and picking her up.

"Mom call the doctor, Sam's going into labor."

Total pandemonium broke out as everyone started talking at once. My only concern was my flower so I left them to figure it out while I headed for my car.

Chief was there before me and I got the two of them situated by the time the rest of the family came out to head to their cars.

"Doc will meet us there son."

I waved and drove away, looking in the rear view mirror I saw chief holding her hand and whispering to her.

My heart was beating me to death, not only because of the labor, but because this was her nightmare, her own mother had died giving birth to her and she was afraid of history repeating itself.

"Baby everything is going to be perfect I promise."

"That's right Samantha listen to Gabriel, he knows what he's talking about."

I could hear the tension in his voice too, hang in there chief, we'll all get through this.

The hospital was more chaos. I left my family to deal with paperwork and whatever while I followed her to the birthing room.

Six hours later we were the proud parents of a baby boy, our little Philip.

THE END

You may contact the author at

Jordansilver144@gmail.com

Jordansilver.net

If you enjoyed this you may also like these works by the author

http://www.amazon.com/dp/B00E0V9ENO

http://www.amazon.com/dp/B00EP1ZZ14

http://www.amazon.com/dp/B00E8HL9WY

http://www.amazon.com/dp/B00EGS7B9K

http://www.amazon.com/dp/B00DQLWDD
W

And many more

Made in the USA
Middletown, DE
02 September 2021

47463080R00156